Sugarland

Ali Spooner

Affinity
eBook Press
NZ
2014

Sugarland
© Ali Spooner 2014

Affinity E-Book Press NZ LTD.
Canterbury, New Zealand

1st Edition

ISBN: 978-1-927282-51-9

Editor: Ruth Stanley
Cover Design: Irish Dragon Designs

Acknowledgements

I would like to thank Affinity Ebook Press, my publisher, and staff for the opportunity to publish this work.

I would also like to thank Cat M. for loving the story encouraging me bring Sasha and Milly to life.

I would also like to thank Terry Baker, whose wonderful reviews continue to inspire me to grow as a writer.

Thank you also to Nancy K. for the beautiful cover art.

To my readers, thank you for supporting me and providing feedback on my stories.

Dedication

Sugarland is dedicated to the memory of Laura, my mother and first hero. Your love will always live in my heart.

Table of Contents

Memories 1
Chapter One—In the Beginning 3
Chapter Two—New York City 14
Chapter Three— 26
Chapter Four— 36
Chapter Five— 44
Chapter Six— 49
Chapter Seven— 61
Chapter Nine— 75
Chapter Ten 85
Chapter Eleven 95
Chapter Twelve 106
Chapter Thirteen 111
Chapter Fourteen 120
Chapter Fifteen 129
Chapter Sixteen 137
Chapter Seventeen 144
Chapter Eighteen 151
Chapter Nineteen 157
Chapter Twenty 164
Chapter Twenty-one 171
Chapter Twenty-two 177
Chapter Twenty-three 185
Chapter Twenty-four 192
Chapter Twenty-five 200
Chapter Twenty-six 205
Chapter Twenty-seven 211
Chapter Twenty-eight 218
About the Author 238
Other Books from Affinity 239

By Ali Spooner

Epitaph
Bailey's Run

Memories

Sasha sat in front of the baby grand piano in the parlor of her Sugarland home, her lavender eyes, framed by raven hair, sparkling with tears. Her fingers caressed the ivory keys as she played a piece by Bach while she focused on the portrait hanging on the wall. A beautiful blond-haired woman with deep blue eyes gazed out of the painting, transfixing Sasha. She willed her mind to relax, as her thoughts traveled back to the day of the photograph, which eventually became the model for the portrait now hanging proudly in her parlor.

"I hope I didn't just break your camera," Milly teased.

"That will probably turn out to be one of the best photographs I have ever taken," Sasha said as she joined her lover. "Are you ready to have our picnic now?"

"Yes, my darling," Milly said.

Milly spread the small blanket beneath the majestic oak and they enjoyed the meal that Martha had packed for them.

"Have I told you yet today how much I love you?" Sasha asked.

"Several times, but I can never hear those words enough," Milly said as she lay down and placed her head in Sasha's lap.

"I love you with all my being and my love for you will last an eternity," Sasha vowed as she bent down to kiss Milly.

1

They had spent the remainder of the afternoon making love beneath the towering oak. When they returned to the horses, Sasha looked at Milly and said, "I will always cherish today's memories. Thank you for creating them with me."

Sasha sighed as her fingers stroked the piano. "Milly, my love, I miss you so."

Over twenty years had passed since Milly's death in the 1980s, yet Sasha still felt the raw pain of her loss. She had witnessed so much death in her life, but nothing had devastated Sasha like the death of her beloved Milly. As she stared back at the deep blue eyes, Sasha could still hear the melodic sound of Milly's laughter as she said, "smile" when Sasha took the photograph so many years ago. Tears flowed down Sasha's cheeks as she remembered the love they had shared and her mind drifted further back, to the very beginning.

Chapter One

In the Beginning

Sasha Thibodaux's parents, Theo and Marie, met and fell in love at a New Orleans social where Marie was performing on a baby grand piano in the fall of 1888. A successful shipping entrepreneur, Theo, drawn by the music, was entranced from his first sight of Marie. A touring concert pianist and proper Cajun woman, Marie's piano performances were a highlight of the bustling socials held by New Orleans' most elite inhabitants. Their courtship began that humid evening and quickly blossomed into a passionate romance.

Their engagement lasted a year and the wedding set a new standard for the New Orleans community. Theo's success afforded him the wealth to purchase a large mansion on the river's east side, where he and Marie made their home.

†

Theo and Marie traveled to Europe for an extended honeymoon. Nearly a month later, on their last night in Paris, they strolled beneath a blanket of stars. As they sat on a nearby bench marveling at the heaven's handiwork, Marie said to Theo, "My love, are you ready to be a father?"

Theo looked at Marie with disbelief. "Are you sure?"

"Very much so," Marie said with a smile. "We are going to have a child."

Theo jumped from his seat and his shouts of joy echoed throughout the vast courtyard. He then took Marie in his arms for a passionate kiss.

"Marie, you are making all my dreams come true," Theo said, nearly breathless.

†

The next day, they began their journey homeward. Marie was plagued by morning sickness on the trip, but Theo remained by his wife's side and attended to her every need.

When they returned to New Orleans, he hired Caroline Dupont, a Cajun midwife, as a companion for Marie. They spent their mornings sipping tea in the gardens and in the parlor where Marie played the piano. After lunch, Marie would retire for a brief nap to refresh herself before Theo's return.

Each night, Theo returned home and placed his hand on his wife's swollen stomach to feel the strong heartbeat of his growing child. He would then gently embrace Marie for a soft kiss, barely able to restrain his excitement as the day of birthing grew closer.

The summer's heat continued to build and on the first day of July, Caroline found Theo in the parlor.

"Marie's time is growing near." Caroline smiled at him. "Are you ready to be a father?"

"I have dreamed of this for nine months, Caroline, I couldn't be more ready," Theo said.

For two days, Caroline sat beside Marie's bed and when her labor began on the third, Theo joined them.

He sat with them through thirty hours of painful labor, refusing to leave her side.

"Does it always take this long?" he asked Caroline.

"The child decides when it is ready and this one seems to be taking its time," Caroline said.

"Is there anything I can get you, my love?" Theo asked as he held Marie's hand.

"No, Theo. Having you here with me as we welcome our child is all I need," Marie managed to say between painful contractions.

Tormented by the pain Marie was experiencing, Theo knew there was nothing he could do to relieve her agony. He sat beside her bed for hours, offering words of comfort. He wiped the perspiration from her face with a cool cloth and spoke to her in soothing tones. "It won't be much longer," he promised as he saw Caroline get into position to receive the child.

"Here we go," Caroline said as the crown of the baby's head became visible. "You have to push now, Marie."

Theo watched as his exhausted wife used the remainder of her strength to expel the baby from her body. When the child was born, Marie passed out from the exertion, causing Theo great worry. "Is this normal?" he asked as he looked at Marie with concern.

"Very much so, Theo, so there is no need to worry. Marie is just exhausted and relieved the process is over."

Theo had watched carefully as Marie gave birth to their daughter. Caroline cleaned and swaddled the baby, then placed her in his arms for the first time as Theo's tears flowed freely.

"You have a beautiful daughter," Caroline said.

"Welcome to the world, Sasha Marie Thibodaux," he said as he cradled the infant near his body.

Marie had opened her eyes again and watched as Theo sat on the edge of the bed, cradling their daughter.

"She is so beautiful, Marie," Theo said as he turned the child so Marie could see her daughter.

The raven-haired infant stole Theo's breath away and he stared in wonder at his daughter.

"She is so beautiful, Marie," Theo repeated.

Marie smiled weakly at her husband. "You look so natural with our daughter."

"That sounds so good, please say it again."

"I said, you look so natural with our daughter," Marie repeated.

"I love you so," Theo said as he leaned down to kiss Marie.

✝

From the day of her birth, Theo vowed to do everything possible to give his daughter the best life had to offer.

During the first few years, Sasha spent her mornings playing in the gardens with Caroline and her mother and the afternoons sitting beside her mother at the piano in the parlor. Sasha was born with her mother's love for music and quickly learned to play, much to her mother's delight.

"Mother," Sasha innocently asked one day, "why don't I have a brother or sister?"

The intense, prolonged labor had left Marie scarred and unable to bear another child.

Marie smiled down at her small child. "Sometimes, Sasha, a child is born so perfect God decides she is all that is needed to complete a family." She ran her hand through Sasha's dark curls and continued. "When you were sent to us, your father and I were complete and no other children were needed."

Sasha mirrored her mother's smile, satisfied with her answer, and returned her fingers to the piano keys.

✝

When Theo realized Sasha would be his sole heir, he became determined to teach her all he could about the world of business.

When she was five, Theo hired a private tutor for Sasha, who proved to be an apt pupil, learning several languages in written and spoken form. By age ten, Sasha was assisting her father with her newly acquired bookkeeping skills as her hunger for knowledge continued to burn.

At sixteen, when it had become evident that Sasha had reached her potential with her tutor, Marie and Theo sat in the parlor one night to discuss Sasha's future.

"Theo, there is a new school opening in New York City, that specializes in Musical Art," Marie said. "I think we should allow Sasha to attend."

"But, New York is so far away," Theo said.

"That is true, but don't you want Sasha to have the very best?"

"You know I do, my love," Theo answered.

"Then New York is the place for our daughter."

Theo and Marie sat up late into the evening debating the issue. Eventually he relented and agreed to allow Sasha to be educated so far from home.

"You are right, Marie, Sasha must have the best education we can provide her," he finally admitted.

†

"Sasha, your father and I have been discussing your continued education, and we want to discuss it with you," Marie said the next day. "There is a new school opening in New York that we feel would be the best place for you."

So much like her father, Sasha said, "But it is so far from home, Mother."

Theo could not help but smile as Sasha's initial response echoed his own.

"We realize that it will be the farthest you have ever been away from home, Sasha, but we want you to have the best education possible," Theo said.

"If you think that is best, Father, then I will go."

Sasha later admitted she was excited about traveling and studying in New York City. That night they made plans to travel to New York City to allow her to audition.

†

Sasha, Theo, and Marie traveled to New York City by train two weeks later. Sasha sat at the windows for hours watching the landscape change as they traveled further north and for the first time she saw mountains and large cities.

"The country is so beautiful," Sasha said to her father as she sat next to him.

"There is so much of the world yet for you to see, Sasha," Theo said. "I hope that in your lifetime you will have the opportunity to see many more marvelous places."

Sasha gasped when New York City came into view. "Is this it, Father?" she asked.

"Welcome to New York City, Sasha," Theo said.

Sasha was overwhelmed with the enormity of New York City at first. However, when she took her first steps on campus, Sasha knew the Institute of Musical Art was where she belonged.

"Are you ready?" Theo asked.

"Yes, Father," Sasha said, then climbed the steps to the stage and sat before a beautiful piano.

Sasha took a deep breath and played to perfection two of the most difficult pieces her mother had taught her. Amazed by the sound of her music in such an acoustically perfect room, the music came to life for Sasha. She finished the last piece, turned on the piano bench, and smiled at her parents. The instructors were speechless as Sasha stood and walked over to her parents.

"Mother, you are right, this is where I need to study," Sasha said while they waited for the instructors' decision.

"We are very impressed with your daughter's talent and would like for Sasha to begin this fall," the Dean of Music told them, offering her a scholarship that she gratefully accepted.

They agreed Sasha would return to New York to begin her studies in the fall, and then went to explore the city she would soon call home.

"This city is so amazing," Sasha said to her mother as they walked through one of the many parks admiring the monuments and statues.

"I'm confident that you will make the most of this opportunity and will have a marvelous time in such a wondrous city," Marie said while they walked back to the hotel.

✝

During her final month in New Orleans, Sasha worked with her father and spent her free time strolling along the streets of the city she loved. One afternoon, Theo found his daughter sitting atop the levee, staring out across the Big Muddy. He sat beside his daughter and in silence they watched the great river flowing by for a while.

Sensing her trepidation, Theo said, "I understand your anxiety, but I know once you arrive in New York, you will blossom."

"I know you're right, Father," Sasha said. "But I will miss home so much."

Theo chuckled. "Nawlins is in your blood and will always be your home, my child, and no big, exciting city will ever change that."

Sasha threw her arms around her father and he held her, so proud of the young woman she was becoming.

"I love you, Father," Sasha whispered.

"I love you, Sasha," Theo replied.

They stood together and walked back toward Theo's office. "There is something I want to show you," Theo said as he locked the door and led Sasha down the sidewalk.

They walked several blocks until they reached one of the oldest of New Orleans' cemeteries. He led her to a raised single crypt with Thibodaux carved into the stone. Looking closer, Sasha could see a smaller name and date.

Sasha Thibodaux
1830—1880

"My mother and your grandmother," Theo said to a wide-eyed Sasha. "You look so much like her that I find it eerie, Sasha. I never knew my father, who died at sea before I was born. Your grandmother raised me alone, in an era when that was extremely difficult." Theo paused for a moment, thoughts of his mother surfacing again after many years. "I can remember her coming home late at night, her hands raw and blistered from the long days of labor necessary for her to raise me."

Sasha could see the tears in his eyes as he continued.

"A stronger woman was never born. She would work long hours and then after a brief sleep, she would wake to check my schoolwork before sending me off to the private school she was struggling to afford." Theo's fingers touched the weatherworn granite. "She died when I was fifteen, but through her sacrifice she gave me the knowledge to make my way in the world. I went to work at the docks and saved every penny I could until I had enough to start a company of my own." Theo looked at Sasha. "You have the inner strength of my mother, and I know you will go to New York and make us proud."

Sasha, who had remained silent, swallowed hard and pushed back her tears. "I will not disappoint you or Grandmother," she promised.

"I know," Theo said, then bent down and kissed the stone above his mother's name.

They walked home in silence, both relishing the time they had spent together.

✝

In two more days, Sasha would leave for New York. She accompanied Theo to the train station to make her arrangements and helped her mother and Caroline pack her trunks for travel.

"Are you sure you don't want us to travel to New York with you to see you settled in?" Theo asked that evening.

"Thank you for offering, Father, but it is time I go out on my own," Sasha said, sounding so grown up to her father.

Theo watched Sasha prepare for her trip. He smiled at his daughter, so pleased at how mature she was for her age, and how blessed they were with a very special child.

✝

The day before her departure, Sasha woke early and went into the garden to pick some flowers. She walked out of the garden gate and allowed her feet to lead her back to the cemetery. She located her grandmother's crypt and laid her offering of flowers on it. Her fingers traced the carved letters of her namesake, and she felt the strength of the

11

woman laid to rest here. "I will make you proud, Grandmother," she said. She sat on a small bench next to the crypt and pondered why her father had waited so long to bring her here.

A shadow fell across the bench and Sasha looked up to see Theo standing next to her. She did not hear his approach and was startled to see him there.

"I wanted you to know the strength from which you were made, and I felt you were ready," Theo said in response to her silent question. He sat beside Sasha. "I wish she had lived long enough to have met you."

"I would have loved that," Sasha said with a smile.

Theo and Sasha sat in the cemetery for hours as he told her stories from his childhood, and made the grandmother she had never met come to life for her. When he finished, Theo kissed the stone. He smiled as Sasha bent down to kiss the stone and whispered, "Goodbye, Grandmother."

Sasha spent the rest of the day at the office with her father. "Who will keep you organized when I am gone?" she asked, teasing her father.

"Well, I will expect you to work double time when you are home on holidays," Theo answered.

Sasha smiled at him and then her expression changed. "What if I don't like school, Father?" she asked.

"I doubt that will happen, but you can always come home and work here with me," he answered.

Sasha took comfort in her father's words as she sat across the desk from him.

Theo quietly opened the desk drawer, pulled out a small gift box, and slid it across the desk. Sasha took the box in her hands, gasping in shock when she opened the lid. Inside was a small golden locket and when she opened it, she found a picture of her parents on the right side and on the left a picture of a woman who had to be her grandmother. "Is this Grandmother?" she asked.

"It is the only photograph of her that was ever taken," Theo answered. "I have carried it with me until now and today I pass it on to you. If you find yourself homesick or in need of comfort, you can look at us to remind you of your strength."

"Thank you, for such a beautiful gift, Father," Sasha said.

"You are very welcome, and I want you to know how proud we are of you," he said with a warm smile.

Sasha looked at the beautiful piece for several minutes and then slipped the chain over her head. The locket rested comfortably on her chest and felt warm against her skin.

†

That night she dreamed of the adventures ahead and woke the next morning to a hearty breakfast. Her parents and Caroline accompanied her to the train station. The tears fell freely, as their daughter began the first of many journeys to come in her life.

"Take good care, my child," Theo said as he kissed Sasha's cheek.

"I will, I promise, Father," Sasha replied.

"Write as often as you can and let us know how school is going," Marie said.

"I promise I will, Mother," Sasha said, swallowing hard against the threatening tears.

Caroline kissed Sasha and handed her a small package. "Open this later," she said. "I still can't believe how fast you have grown up." She sighed and shook her head.

Sasha laughed softly. "I will see you all soon," she said and climbed onto the train.

Chapter Two

New York City

Sasha finished dinner in the dining car and then remained in the passenger section for several more hours until the sun dipped below the horizon. She retired to the sleeping cabin and lay on the cot, watching the dark clouds as they passed before a glowing harvest moon. Eventually, the gentle rocking of the car on the tracks lulled her to sleep and she dreamed of her grandmother.

†

When she woke the next morning, Sasha could barely remember dreaming as she dressed and made her way to the dining car for breakfast. Midmorning the train crossed into Virginia and during a stop to collect additional passengers, Sasha left the train to get some exercise. She stepped into a bright sunny morning, filled with the aromas of fruit. The farmers brought it in fresh from the orchards to the farmers market located next to the train station. Sasha bought two large yellow apples from a merchant and walked the market aisles until the conductor announced it was time again to board the train.

She savored the sweetness of the apple as she watched the countryside rolling by, the train devouring mile after mile of track. Sasha marveled at a small waterfall, nestled into the cleavage of a mountain, and imagined bathing in the cool, clear water. Such beauty she had never imagined so far from her home. The rivers and bayous were almost alien compared to the rolling valleys and deeply colored mountains she was passing through. The richness of the colored foliage in particular pleased Sasha, who had never witnessed the change of the seasons. She loved the ancient oaks and moss-covered cypresses of home, but they were astonishingly different from the elms and maples burning with color.

Sasha also felt a cold crispness in the air, so unlike the humid air which hung thickly in New Orleans. She observed her fellow passengers, who, unlike herself, appeared oblivious to the beauty surrounding them.

When Sasha retired for the evening, she opened the small package Caroline had given her, finding a small, leather-bound notebook. She wrote in the small diary, capturing her thoughts and sights of the day. Caroline had made Sasha promise to make frequent entries to document her journey. When she had finished her notes, Sasha tucked the treasured book into her bag and slipped quietly between the sheets. Now accustomed to the movement of the train, Sasha drifted off to a peaceful sleep.

†

When she awoke the next morning, Sasha peered out the frosted window and saw a sign noting the mileage to New York City to be five more miles. Sasha freshened up and packed away her traveling clothes as the final miles slipped away.

Sasha stepped off the train, made her way through the throng of travelers, and saw an older black man standing beside a horse-drawn carriage just outside the station. He approached her and politely asked, "Are you Miss Thibodaux?"

"Yes, sir," Sasha said to the warmly smiling man.

15

"My name is Joshua, and I have been sent from the Alyson Boarding House to collect you and your trunks," the man said in his rich, deep voice.

"Why thank you, sir," Sasha said as she handed Joshua the bag she was carrying.

Joshua led Sasha to the carriage and placed her in the comfortable seat. "I will collect your trunks and we will be on our way," Joshua said before he disappeared into the crowd of passengers bustling to retrieve their baggage.

After a while Joshua returned, loaded the three trunks Sasha had traveled with and then climbed onto the driver's seat of the carriage. He picked up the reins, and with a soft clicking sound and a gentle slap of the reins against the horse's neck they were off.

Joshua remained silent, allowing Sasha to take in the sights of the bustling city, now awake with hundreds of people rushing back and forth as they hurried to tend to their business. When they arrived at the boarding house, Sasha was ushered into her new home by Mary, who was the owner of the establishment. She handed Sasha a key as well as a list of the rules and meal times for the boarding house and then swiftly departed, leaving a dazzled Sasha standing in the middle of a large room.

Sasha spent the afternoon putting away her clothing and arranging her room. She was pleased that there was a small desk in front of the room's sole window. She could study there while looking out over a small wooded park. Checking the time, Sasha saw it was time for dinner and made her way down to the dining room.

She took a seat at the long table, and Mary introduced her to the other five young women sitting around the table. They were all students of the Institute who would be starting classes with her on Monday. Joshua and his wife Ella served a lovely meal of pork roast, fresh vegetables, and fresh-baked yeast rolls. Sasha joined in on the friendly banter around the table and immediately felt drawn to the blond girl named Amelia from Atlanta, sitting to her right. The other girls, mostly from the Northeast or Midwest, chuckled at the southern drawl spoken by both Amelia and Sasha as if they were speaking in a foreign language. Having been properly raised as Southern women, neither Sasha nor Amelia commented on the strange accents of the others, though their speech sounded like rabid chipmunks prattling along.

Sasha leaned over and whispered to Amelia. "I am so relieved there is someone else from the South here." Amelia grinned back in answer. Sasha was even more pleased to find that Amelia's room was next to hers and there was a small doorway between the rooms. They spent the rest of the evening excitedly discussing their enrollment at the Institute, and they agreed to meet again after breakfast to spend the day exploring their new surroundings. Sasha pulled her diary from her desk and made a brief entry before checking the bathing room to see if it was vacant.

Fortunately, it was, and Sasha started to draw the water before she went back to her room for her nightgown and towel. When she returned, she poured a small amount of lavender scent into the water and stepped into a hot bath. The lavender scent reminded her of the garden at home and for a moment, she drifted into melancholy thoughts. Her fingers grazed the locket on her neck, reminding her to remove it. She set it beside the tub and then smiled to herself and lay back to enjoy her bath. Sasha returned to her room completely relaxed, turned off the gas lamp, and slid between cool, soft sheets to dream her night away.

†

The next morning, Sasha heard a light tap on the door adjoining her room and Amelia's. She opened the door to greet her new friend. "Good morning, Amelia."

"Good morning, Sasha. I am so excited to be exploring the city today," Amelia said.

"Well, let's go see what Ella has for breakfast and we will be off for the day," Sasha said.

†

Refreshed and fueled with a hearty breakfast, Sasha and Amelia left the boarding house to begin their exploration. They first discovered the route they would need to take the following day to the Institute and then fanned out from there, walking several blocks in each direction, noting bakeries, dress shops, a small museum of fine art and several parks.

During their exploration, Sasha discovered that Amelia was a violinist who was also sixteen and away from home for the first time. She was quick to speak her mind and rapidly became Sasha's best friend. The "Belles," as they would soon be nicknamed, were almost inseparable, spending their free time together whenever possible.

Later, much to the delight of their instructors, their friendship extended to include their music and they frequently practiced together.

†

"That is such a beautiful piece," Sasha said to Amelia one day as they ended a practice session.

"I thought you might recognize it," Amelia replied. "I heard you playing it a few weeks ago and decided I would practice the piece as well."

"I would say you have definitely tapped into the passion of the music then," Sasha said. "You play it so beautifully."

"Thank you, Sasha," Amelia said. She respected Sasha's opinion and was proud to receive a compliment from her friend, knowing it was how she truly felt.

Amelia and Sasha, unlike most of their classmates, were serious about their music. The majority of the other young women were only interested in learning parlor music and landing a fine husband, but the two young friends craved to learn more about music. Together they would spend hours practicing while their peers would be out socializing and enjoying their youth.

Sasha's fingers would glide across the ivory as she watched Amelia, eyes closed, caressing the violin with her bow as their notes danced in the air. Frequently, they would find themselves playing the same practice piece, their efforts joining in beautiful harmony as they became lost in the magic of their music.

For their midterm examination, they would perform a classic selection assigned by their instructor and compose an original piece. Both excelled in performance, but Amelia struggled with composition.

"Oh, Sasha, I will never get this piece written," Amelia declared one afternoon.

"With my help you will," Sasha said and moved over next to Amelia.

Sasha tutored her friend in writing the piece and selecting the tempo of the music. They labored together for several hours.

"There, I think we have it now," Sasha said as she smiled at Amelia. "Try it now."

Amelia picked up her bow and violin and began to play the piece they had composed. Sasha sat with her eyes closed as she listened with a critical ear to the music Amelia played.

When she finished, Amelia asked, "What do you think?"

Sasha opened her eyes and smiled at her friend. "I think you have created a perfect piece of music for your violin."

†

Amelia and Sasha practiced endlessly as they prepared for their exams.

Both she and Amelia remained in New York City over Thanksgiving to practice their performances. Joshua and Ella created a terrific Thanksgiving meal for them, complete with sweet potato and pecan pies. After enjoying the feast, Sasha and Amelia opted for a walk.

Thanking the couple for the lovely meal, the young women, wrapped in thick coats, stepped out to an overcast afternoon. They walked the streets for an hour before deciding to return home. The temperature dropped quickly and moisture from the heavy clouds that hovered above them escaped to form the first snowflakes Sasha had ever seen.

"Can you believe this? We have snow!" Sasha shouted as she raced circles around Amelia.

Amelia laughed as Sasha chased the flakes that melted in her hands as she giggled and danced down the sidewalk. When they returned to the boarding house, Sasha sat at her desk for hours watching the flakes fall softly as they began to accumulate on the ground. Finally exhausted, Sasha succumbed to sleep.

†

A light tapping at the adjoining door woke Sasha the next morning, and when she opened it, Amelia grabbed her hand and rushed her to the window. Sasha gasped at the beauty of the small park blanketed by the bright snow. Limbs that were until recently covered by beautifully colored leaves were now enveloped by the stark white snow. The view of the winter blanket was breathtaking to Sasha.

"Have you ever seen anything so beautiful?" she asked.

"Believe it or not, we have had snow in Georgia before. It doesn't keep me from wanting to go out and play in it though," she said as she pushed Sasha back onto her bed and ran from the room laughing.

They rushed to dress and bundled up before stepping outside to the crunch of the snow under their feet. Sasha bent to scoop a handful of the frozen liquid in her hands and quickly learned to make her first snowball, which she promptly tossed at Amelia, striking her on the shoulder. The battle was on, Amelia fired a snowball back at Sasha, and for nearly a half hour they chased one another until the cold and their exhaustion forced them back inside.

Ella, who had stood at the window watching the "Belles" frolicking in the snow, prepared fresh biscuits and thick gravy for their breakfast. Their good manners and heartfelt thanks had made Amelia and Sasha her favorites of the new batch of boarders, and Ella did her best to make them feel at home.

"That was a great breakfast," Sasha said. "Just like home."

"I am glad that you two enjoy my cooking so much. The others don't seem to appreciate it," Ella said.

"I think they are too busy choking on their silver spoons to appreciate your cooking, Ella," Sasha said.

"Sasha!" Amelia exclaimed. "How rude of you to say that."

Sasha looked at Ella then at Amelia and burst into laughter.

"It may not be proper, missy, but it is the truth," Sasha said with a cheerful wink to Ella.

They spent the rest of the day sitting by the fireplace, drinking hot cocoa and talking with Ella and Joshua.

✝

The weeks passed quickly and Theo and Marie arrived in town for the Christmas Concert performance, along with Amelia's parents from Georgia. The two families dined together in the city and sat together during the concert. Both sets of parents were proud of their daughters, who were the highlight of the show. Sasha and Amelia performed individually and then together as the grand finale of the show. It was obvious to the entire audience that they were the premier artists of the school, their skills much more advanced than even those of the older students. The theater buzzed with excitement after their performance and their parents' chests swelled with pride.

✝

For four years, Sasha and Amelia studied together at the Institute, and traveled throughout the Northeast performing concerts for the Institute. All was well until the end of their fourth year when Amelia's father called her home. Her mother had taken ill and her father needed her assistance in raising her younger siblings. Their plans to travel to London to study at King's College together would have to wait as Amelia attended to her family's needs.

When Amelia told Sasha of the news, Sasha hugged her tightly. "Everything will work out for the best," she said as she wiped the tears from her friend's cheek.

On their last night together, Sasha and Amelia walked the streets of New York, reliving the times they had shared and then sat in Sasha's room for hours talking about London.

"I am so excited about going to London with you," Amelia said.

"I know, I almost wish we could leave right away," Sasha said.

"The summer will pass quickly and we will be bound for London before you know it," Amelia said as she draped her arm around Sasha's shoulders.

When Amelia stood to return to her room, Sasha embraced her friend. She could see the tears welling in Amelia's eyes, and without hesitation, Sasha gently placed her lips on Amelia's for a soft kiss.

"I love you, Amelia," Sasha said to her shocked friend. "Your mother will recover quickly and before you know it, we will be entertaining the royal city of London with our musical talents."

Amelia hugged Sasha tight and whispered, "I love you, too," and then left the room before she broke down in tears.

Sasha stretched across her bed as she contemplated her future. Her feelings for Amelia confused Sasha. She knew the desires she felt every time she looked at Amelia were unnatural, desires only shared between a man and his wife. Unnatural or not, Sasha felt as if her heart would leap out of her chest as she lay thinking of kissing Amelia, her mind racing with excitement as she dreamed of a more intimate relationship with her. Every time they touched, Sasha felt a giddy rush of excitement run through her and her body quivered with desire. Sasha knew their touches were growing beyond playful kisses and she looked forward to deepening their relationship while they were abroad. While Sasha had never shared the truth of her feelings with Amelia, she was certain Amelia felt a love that was beyond mere friendship. Sasha fell asleep that night dreaming of the times she and Amelia would share once they sailed for Europe.

✝

The next morning, Sasha tapped lightly on Amelia's door. She pushed the door open and found Amelia sitting on the edge of the bed, crying. She rushed to her friend and knelt down in front of her. "I know you are disappointed, but right now your family needs you," Sasha said.

"Have faith that all will work out as it should be, my friend," she added as she lifted Amelia's chin. "Are you all set?"

Amelia wiped the tears from her eyes and nodded her head. "Yes, I am ready."

Sasha and Joshua accompanied her to the train station. Joshua took her trunks to be loaded onto the train as Amelia and Sasha shared a private goodbye. With eyes filled with tears, they promised to write and keep in touch while they were apart.

"I will miss you so," Amelia said.

"Keep in touch, and if you think your mother is well enough, I will try to come to Georgia for a visit," Sasha said. Sasha saw the tears in Amelia's eyes and felt her own rising quickly.

With a final hug, Amelia turned away from Sasha and boarded the train for home.

Joshua remained silent on the ride back to the boarding house, knowing how much Sasha was already missing Amelia.

When they returned to the boarding house, Joshua helped Sasha down from the carriage.

"Don't fret, Miss Sasha. In no time at all the Belles will be together again. I just hope London is ready for the two of you," he said with a warm smile.

Sasha took comfort from his gentle words. "I hope you are right, Joshua," she said and with a sigh, entered the house.

For the next three days, Sasha moped around the house as she packed her belongings for her trip home. She would spend the summer in New Orleans working with her father, before sailing to London in the fall.

Chapter Three

Heartbreak

The absence of Amelia for the train ride muted Sasha's excitement. Normally, had circumstances been different, Amelia would have ridden as far south as Atlanta with Sasha. Nonetheless, Sasha was going home, having graduated at the top of her class and with plans to travel to London to continue her studies at King's College. The education and exposure Sasha could receive in Europe would far surpass what she could obtain in the United States. Her mother had convinced her that all the prominent musicians spent much of their time performing at the various venues in Europe, and Sasha should be no exception.

†

Two days later when the train arrived in New Orleans, Sasha found her father pacing the platform awaiting her return. He hugged his daughter tightly when she stepped down from the train and paid a steward to deliver her bags later that day.

"I have missed you so," Theo said.

"It feels great to be home, and I missed you too, Father."

Sasha reached for her father's hand and they walked home, allowing Sasha to stretch her travel-weary legs. It had been nearly six months since she was home for

Christmas and she was shocked when they entered the house. Her mother's raven hair had deep streaks of gray running through it. Sasha did not comment, but silently she worried about her mother's health.

Caroline was no longer living in the house; instead, she had married and was raising a child of her own. Marie said that she visited often and would bring her son James with her to play in the gardens, just as Sasha had when she was young. The memory of those long days in the garden brought a smile to Sasha's face.

"It seems so strange, not having Caroline here," Sasha commented.

"I am sure you will see plenty of Caroline over the summer," Marie said.

"Caroline has been such a good friend to you, Mother, what would you do without her?" Sasha asked.

"She is the best friend I have ever had," Marie said. "I don't know what I would do without her. I pray it will be many years before I have to find out."

When she climbed the stairs and opened the door to her room, Sasha realized how much she had matured while she was in New York. Still, the memories of her childhood warmed her heart as she looked at the pictures of her parents and herself on holidays and a picture of her parents' wedding that graced the bureau. Sasha's trunks had been shipped a week prior to her leaving New York. Her bags had been delivered from the depot while she and Theo walked home. She spent the afternoon unpacking her trunks and then went downstairs to join her parents for dinner.

†

"Are you and Amelia excited about your trip to London?" Theo asked during dinner.

"I am afraid Amelia's journey may be delayed, Father. Her mother has taken ill and she was called home early from school to care for her siblings," Sasha explained.

Theo and Marie were disappointed to learn of Amelia's mother's ill health. They knew Amelia was important to their daughter and hoped she would continue with her plans to travel to Europe.

"Do you still plan to go to London this fall, even if Amelia cannot join you?" Theo asked.

"Yes, Father, I am committed to King's College, starting in September, and, if all goes well, Amelia will follow whenever possible," she answered.

Relieved by her decision, Theo cheerily talked about the honeymoon he and Marie had spent in Europe. "I am convinced you will fall in love with Europe just as we did," Theo said.

Marie was smiling as she listened to Theo. "It was a memorable time for us, and it was also when you were conceived," she added. "I can still hear your father's shouts echoing in the courtyard when I told him that he would be a father."

"A little excited were you, Father?" Sasha teased.

"I could not wait for you to be born," Theo admitted, the excitement still ringing in his voice.

Sasha chuckled at her father. "He is telling the truth," Marie said. "When I finally went into labor he refused to leave my side, afraid that he would miss your grand entrance."

Theo laughed but did not deny Marie's claim. He was a proud father then and now as he looked at his daughter across the table. What a fine young woman she had grown into, he thought.

"You came into this world as perfection and have not missed a beat," Theo said to his daughter.

"I think you are just a little biased, Father, but thank you," Sasha said. "Would you two mind if I took a walk? I feel like I still need to stretch my legs."

"No, not at all," Theo said, sensing his daughter's sadness.

†

Sasha took a walk down by the levee. As the sun sank below the horizon, she thought of Amelia and wondered how she was faring with her mother's illness. She would write a letter to her tonight to let her know that she was thinking of her and wishing her mother well. With a deep sigh of loneliness, Sasha returned to the house and bid her parents goodnight, then disappeared into her room.

When she pulled out paper and ink to write to Amelia, Sasha found it hard to find the words she wanted to say. She missed her close friend terribly and hoped they could be together again soon, but every time she started to write, the words she wrote were stiff and without the warmth she felt whenever she thought of Amelia. She resolved to send a brief note with well wishes to her mother and a plea for Amelia to write soon or visit if possible. Sasha wrote Amelia's address on the envelope and put it on her nightstand. She would take it to post the next morning before joining her father in the office.

†

The weeks of that summer passed quickly. Sasha spent her days working with her father, teasing him endlessly at how disheveled the office had become without her supervision. Each day she would return home with him to find that no letter had arrived from Amelia and her worry began to grow. Finally, two weeks before she was to sail to

London, Sasha walked into the foyer to see a letter lying on the table. She picked it up and walked out to the garden. Sitting beneath a shadowy willow, Sasha opened the letter from Amelia. The further she read, the more her heart broke. Amelia's mother had made an almost complete recovery from her illness, which was a relief to the entire family. However, Amelia wrote that she was in love with the young, handsome doctor who had nursed her mother back to health and announced they would be married on October 1.

The letter fell from Sasha's hand into her lap as she struggled to hold back her tears. Amelia was in love with someone else, and she would marry when Sasha would not be able to attend. Unable to control her heartbreak, Sasha's tears rolled freely down her cheeks.

She remained in the garden and read over Amelia's letter several times, her anger toward Amelia growing furiously. She felt her friend had betrayed their love, and the more Sasha dwelled on the letter, the angrier she became. All those promises made were just empty words to Sasha as she balled up Amelia's letter in her hand. "Damn you, Amelia," Sasha said as her tears returned. Sasha wallowed in her bitterness, and disappointment until the sun began to set, then she walked inside and climbed the steps to her room.

✝

Theo had peeked out the window to look at Sasha several times during the afternoon and wanted to go to his daughter. He knew some bad news had been contained in the letter and he wanted to protect his daughter from the hurt she must be feeling. When Theo couldn't stand his daughter's heartbreak any longer, he headed for the door.

"Theo," Marie called to him.

"Yes, my love?"

"Let her be for now until she has had a chance to sort out her feelings," Marie said.

"But, I can't stand to see her cry," Theo said.

"I know, but Sasha is a young woman now and there will be many more tears in her future," Marie said. "She has to deal with them on her own and will come to us when she needs our advice."

Theo walked over to kiss Marie. "I know you are right, but still my heart goes out to her," he said.

"You have been a compassionate father," Marie said, "but she must deal with these feelings on her own."

Marie's words did not stop Theo from walking to the window periodically to peer out at Sasha while she sat in the garden. He returned to reading his newspaper, and when the door from the garden opened and closed, he looked up in time to see Sasha rush up the stairs to her room. His heart ached to go to Sasha and soothe away the hurt and anger she was feeling, but his common sense and the look he got from Marie kept him in his seat.

†

That evening, the words poured from Sasha's pen as she wrote to Amelia, telling her how pleased she was for Amelia and her fiancé. Her anger finally subsiding, Sasha wished the two of them the best of luck. Sasha realized that Amelia could never know how much the news broke her heart. The love she had for Amelia was pointless now, but Sasha could not bear to see her in love with anyone else. As painful as it was, Sasha knew this would be the last time she would correspond to the woman who had meant so much to her, and when she sealed the envelope, Sasha knew another chapter of her life had ended.

✝

Sasha found solace in visiting her grandmother's crypt when life's hardships closed in around her, and she found herself walking to the cemetery after posting her letter to Amelia. She sat beside her grandmother's crypt and drew strength from the woman laid to rest there. Sasha understood that her grandmother would have felt the terrible pain of losing a love when her husband was lost at sea and somehow she had the fortitude to continue to raise Theo alone, never remarrying or relying on others for assistance. Sasha knew she would survive the heartache of losing Amelia, and walk the path fate had set before her feet.

Though she struggled with the knowledge that she would be traveling alone in Europe, Sasha remained focused on her goals and would not allow her separation from Amelia to become an obstacle. She was young, and she knew there would be many more adventures to come in her life. Forcing a smile, Sasha stood and walked to her father's office to begin her day.

✝

As Sasha settled behind her desk, Theo sensed a change in his daughter, but knew her well enough to know that if she wanted to talk, she would come to him. Sasha spent the entire day setting up billing invoices for the next few months and when it was time to head home for the evening, Theo had to prompt her that it was time to go.

"Sasha, it is time for us to head home. Your mother will be putting dinner on the table soon and you know how she frets if we are late," he teased.

Immersed in her work she had lost all sense of the time passing.

"Just one more minute, Father," Sasha said as she filed the last invoice. Shutting the drawer, Sasha looked up at her father and smiled. "There, I am ready now."

Theo draped his arm protectively around Sasha's shoulder as they walked. "Father, why is the human heart so fragile?" she asked.

"The best answer I can determine is that for the heart to remain soft and tender enough to fall deeply in love, it must remain vulnerable. When love is betrayed or fails to blossom, the heart temporarily abandons the idea of love and the hurt occurs." Theo sighed deeply and continued. "The strong heart mends itself quickly and grows stronger, though it remains vulnerable to hurt and heartache, for the only other option is to grow distant and cold, unable to love as the heart was intended."

Sasha contemplated his words as they walked toward home. She realized her father was right, and though her wounded heart would take some time to heal, she would become stronger and better prepared for the next time she fell in love.

Sasha slipped her arm through Theo's and they walked in silence until they arrived home. Theo then turned to his daughter and said, "I know Amelia meant the world to you, but her loss will set you on the path to find the one that is right for you."

"I know you are right, Father. I just have to keep telling my heart that until I can convince it that life will go on, and I will find love again," she said as she pushed through the door. "Thank you, Father."

"For what am I receiving your thanks?" Theo asked.

"For being the best father I could ever ask for," Sasha said.

Theo was glad that Sasha had chosen that moment to embrace him. The brief moment allowed him to brush back the tears that had filled his eyes and threatened to roll down his cheeks.

"I am so very proud of you, Sasha," Theo said as he stroked the top of his daughter's head.

"I was starting to get worried about you two," Marie said as she stepped into the hallway when she heard the door open. Witnessing the tender moment between father and daughter, Marie chose to rescue her loving husband from the tears that threatened to fall.

"I told you she would be fretting," Theo teased Sasha. "It's all Sasha's fault. We could have been here earlier, but she felt it necessary to create invoices for the next year or two."

"You had better be thankful she has been there to get you organized again, my love," Marie teased her husband.

"Hah, that backfired on you, didn't it, Father?" Sasha asked.

"I reckon it did at that. So what's for dinner?" he asked to change the subject.

✝

The day arrived for Sasha's departure for London. After tender farewells to her family, she boarded the train that would carry her to New York, from where she would sail across the Atlantic. Though she had made the trip many times during her studies at the Institute, Sasha still loved the route the train traveled. The train stopped briefly in Atlanta to take on additional passengers, and Sasha remembered the times she had waited for Amelia to board the train so they could travel to New York to continue their studies. Sasha felt a sharp pang of heartache as she realized those days was long gone and she was moving on with her life. She regretted that Amelia would not be joining her, but

34

Sasha was excited about the prospects awaiting her in Europe.

†

When she reached New York City, Joshua and Ella met her at the train station and drove her to the harbor. Sasha was happy to see the married couple who had made her stay in New York City so pleasant and wished for a moment they could join her in London.

"It seems like forever since you have been here," Ella said as she hugged Sasha tightly. "I hope that when you have a chance to return home, you will spend a night or two with us."

"You can bet I will," Sasha said.

Ella had packed Sasha a bag of sandwiches and fruit for her trip and after a tearful goodbye, Sasha boarded the ship.

Chapter Four

London and Beyond

The crossing of the vast ocean would take nearly five days and aside from the deep blue waters, there was little for Sasha to see. She spent several hours writing in her diary each day, a new volume to start a new journey. The pages of the first diary Caroline had given her before traveling to New York City she filled and packed away in her trunk, safeguarding her memories from that era. The serenity of the ocean also inspired her to compose several new pieces and she was eager to sit at a piano to play them.

The screeching of the gulls alerted her to the proximity of land and when she looked off the starboard deck, she could see the first land she had seen in days. Her heart raced in her chest as she gathered her small travel bag and waited for the ship to reach port. The ocean liner would dock in Liverpool, and Sasha would spend the remainder of the day traveling south by train on the final leg of her journey to London.

✝

Sasha settled into the stiff seat on the train and waited for the luggage to be loaded. When the train finally blew its whistle and the wheels began to churn, she leaned over to stare out the window at the English countryside. The rolling hills and lush valleys were reminiscent of her train trips to

New York, but instead of cattle and crops, sheep dotted the lush valleys.

The sun was fading quickly as the train pulled into the London train station and she hoped she would arrive at the hotel before nightfall.

Sasha took a carriage ride to the Jolly Saint Ermins, which would be her home at least for the beginning of her life in London. It was a quaint stone building, which held the promise of a sanctuary from the warm days in the summer, but would probably remain chilly in the winter months. Nonetheless, she smiled as she entered her first home in London.

Sasha unpacked her trunks and made her way to the dining room for a light dinner before retiring for the evening. She melted into the soft linens and slept until the morning sun crept through her window.

✝

Sasha was eager to be outside exploring the vast city of London. She located King's College and spent several hours touring the facilities with one of the students as her tour guide. Classes would begin the following week, which would allow Sasha plenty of time to explore.

Though she would get lost several times her first few days in the city, Sasha would discover many fascinating places. The Royal Albert Hall in Westminster was one of the locations she found during one of her adventures. She opened the doors and stepped inside the wondrous concert hall where her mother had performed in her youth. Sasha was surprised to find a piano set up on the stage. Her curiosity ignited, Sasha stepped on the stage and sat at the piano. As her fingers stroked the smooth ivory, her heart raced at the purity of the sound as it vibrated through the acoustically perfect hall.

"What a beautiful sound," a deep, but feminine voice projected across the darkened theater.

Sasha startled and looked in the direction she thought the voice had come. "I am sorry for intruding, but I could not resist testing the acoustics in such a wondrous hall," Sasha admitted.

"'Tis a pleasure and no intrusion to hear such beautiful music," the voice answered from across the stage.

Sasha strained to get a glimpse of the person behind such a rich, sultry voice, but the lighting failed to illuminate any figure. She stood up from the bench and began to walk off the stage, intending to make an exit from the stage into stronger light when she sensed movement to her left. Her eyes focused on a tall, fair-haired woman who had stepped from behind the stage curtain onto the opposite end of the stage.

"I am sorry for my intrusion," Sasha began.

"Nonsense, young lady," the woman answered, a smile crossing her face as she approached Sasha.

"Please pardon my ill manners and let me introduce myself," she said. "My name is Millicent Vansant, and I am a part-time curator of this great hall, as well as a struggling painter and instructor at King's College in the fine arts division."

"I am Sasha Thibodaux, from America, and I have traveled here to study at King's."

"Ah, a Yank then, and from the sound of it, one from one of the southern states as well," Millicent said.

"Yes, I hail from New Orleans," Sasha said with a chuckle.

"Welcome to our city," Millicent said as she moved beside Sasha.

Sasha felt drawn to the ocean-blue eyes that were studying her closely. She felt those eyes penetrating her exterior and searching down to the very core of her being.

38

She struggled to maintain the beating of her heart as the woman moved closer, within arm's reach if Sasha were to extend her hand.

The woman smiled warmly at her and asked, "So, Miss Thibodaux, where are you being housed in our great city?"

"I am staying at the Jolly Saint Ermins," Sasha answered.

"That is quite a walk from here," Millicent said.

"I know, I have been doing some exploring to learn my way around the city," Sasha said.

"It is getting late, and it is not safe for a young woman to be on these streets alone at night, especially one who is not familiar with her surroundings," Millicent said. "I have a flat not too far from where you are staying, and would like to offer to walk with you, if I may."

"That would be lovely," Sasha replied.

"Let me lock up and we will be on our way," Millicent said as she led Sasha back through the hall.

The light was rapidly failing as they stepped out onto the street. "The sun in London has a will of its own and frequently departs before we are ready to be left in the cool darkness," Millicent said as they began to walk. "I have access to a small carriage and I have no plans for tomorrow, if you would be interested in a proper tour of London."

"I would enjoy that," Sasha said.

Their arms brushed together several times as they walked and Sasha felt a warm tingling pass through her whenever their skin touched. She was disappointed when she saw the lights of Saint Ermins ahead, knowing they would soon be parting ways.

"May I offer you some dinner?" Sasha asked, reluctant to see Millicent go.

"Thank you for your offer, but I must decline tonight, due to a previous engagement," Millicent replied. "I will be here at nine, if that is not too early for you."

"Nine will be perfect, and thank you for walking me home, Millicent," Sasha said.

"Milly, please call me Milly," she said in reply.

"Milly it is then," Sasha said with a smile. "I will see you at nine." She watched as Milly disappeared into the misty night.

Sasha reluctantly stepped into the dining room alone. During her dinner, her thoughts kept returning to Milly and the strange feelings this woman had stirred inside her. They were similar to the feelings Sasha had experienced with Amelia and her heart felt the familiar ache whenever she thought of her friend. She pushed the sad thoughts away and concentrated on the many guests in the dining hall. There were several single travelers and a few families enjoying the hot meal, and Sasha listened to the chatter as she dined, unaware of the fact that the woman she had recently met was a very special person indeed.

†

Milly turned around once she had reached the cover of the falling mist and watched as Sasha witnessed her departure and then stepped inside the hotel. What a beautiful young woman, she thought as she watched Sasha disappear. She smiled to herself as she remembered the way the young woman's heart had raced each time the skin of their arms touched as they walked. Using her supernatural powers, Milly had delved into Sasha's thoughts as they talked in the hall and she was pleased that she was attracted to her, even if on a basic level. Milly walked the remaining blocks to her flat, fearless of the danger lurking in the dark alleys, knowing she could easily overcome any would-be attacker. She could hear the many heartbeats of people she passed and she felt the fire of hunger burn inside her, spurred by the desire that was growing for the young Yank.

Milly continued on to her flat, knowing she would return to the streets later that night to feast on an unfortunate soul that would cross her path.

✝

Sasha selected a dress for the next day's tour and ordered up a bath. Soaking in the hot water, she allowed her mind to relax and quickly found Milly buried in her thoughts. Sasha could feel her nipples harden to chiseled peaks as she listened to Milly's voice playing repeatedly in her head. Sasha turned off the light and slipped between the cool sheets after finishing her bath, thoughts of Milly still burning in her mind.

✝

Milly prepared a picnic lunch of cheese, crusty breads, and a bottle of fine wine for the following day, when she would give Sasha her promised tour of the city. She left her flat to feed her hunger and found herself walking back toward Jolly Saint Ermins. She sat on the stone wall in the foggy night and allowed her mind to search out Sasha. She located her room and smiled when she saw the light in her room go dim and then extinguish.

Milly could hear the strong beating of Sasha's heart and listened to the blood rush through her veins as she felt the heat of sexual desire burning in the young woman's body. Focusing on Sasha's thoughts, Milly eavesdropped into her mind and experienced the sensations Sasha felt as her hands roamed across her desire-heated skin. Milly had to stifle a moan as she felt Sasha's hand move further down her body, parting her soaked lower lips. Milly could feel and taste the sweetness of the wetness as Sasha's fingers

41

dipped in and out of her body, her thoughts visualizing Milly's fingers driving deep inside her.

Milly could feel her wetness grow and her hunger burned furiously inside her. She would take this young woman as her lover, and in time perhaps, they would become much more. She waited until Sasha's fingers brought her body to its peak and listened as she whispered Milly's name until she cried out with pleasure.

Confident that Sasha would be hers for the taking, Milly smiled and resumed her hunt. She would prowl through the harbor district and with luck stumble across a sailor with a pint too many in his system. Such easy prey for her, they could be disguised as a drowning victim with little risk of exposure. Milly watched as a young man stumbled toward her. She went to offer him her shoulder for support as she led him down a dark alley.

"'Ello, pretty lady," the young man mumbled.

"Good evening," Milly said as she draped his arm around her shoulder.

"Out for a stroll tonight are ye?" he slurred as his hand slid down to cover Milly's breast.

Repulsed by his touch, Milly quickly withdrew his hand and said, "I am out for a hunt."

"Well, if it's a strapping young man you are searching for, you have found your man," he confidently said.

"That is exactly what I am looking for," Milly said as she sat him down on a small seawall. She leaned over the seated man who thought she was approaching for a kiss, but instead of searching out his lips, Milly turned his head to the side and located his jugular. Fangs exposed, Milly sunk them deep into the man's neck. He fainted from the shock and Milly drank freely from the prostrate man's body as she fed the hunger burning deep inside her. She listened as his heartbeat raced briefly and then began to decline as she took the life from his body. She finished her feast and softly licked the wound in his neck until the skin healed itself. Milly then quietly lowered his lifeless body into the briny water of the harbor.

When he failed to return to his ship the following morning, his body would be found floating in the harbor. He'd be mistaken for another drunken drowning victim. There would be no further need for assumption of any other sort by the authorities, and Milly's feeding would again go unnoticed.

Sated for the moment by the young man's blood, Milly returned to her flat, her hunger satisfied, but a burning desire for Sasha growing deep inside her. She sat in front of the small fireplace as she sipped a glass of wine and her thoughts returned to Sasha. Her mind returned to Sasha's room, and she could hear the soft breathing as Sasha rested quietly.

Refreshed from her feeding, Milly sat and waited for the return of the sun. Her body did not often need sleep, and she spent the early morning hours sketching her first memory of Sasha as she played the piano in the hall, her eyes closed as she reveled in the sound of the music she made. Milly would request to have Sasha sit for a painting, which would take hours to perfect, giving them plenty of time to spend together while being acquainted.

Chapter Five

Westminster Gardens

Milly arrived promptly a few minutes before nine the next morning and was pleased to find Sasha waiting for her. Sasha smiled and waved when she noticed her arrival and quickly walked to the carriage. Milly offered her strong hand and assisted Sasha in climbing into the carriage. Graced by the warm sun, they began their tour of London.

Milly was extremely knowledgeable and passionate about London. She took pride in sharing the city's history with Sasha as the horse pulled them around the city streets at a leisurely pace. They drove past Buckingham Palace and continued to Westminster Gardens, where Milly located a spot that would be perfect for a private picnic lunch. She tied the horse and helped Sasha down from the carriage. She then handed Sasha a thick quilt and picked up the basket filled with their lunch. They walked into the verdant forest and spread the quilt under an ancient sprawling tree. Milly opened the bottle of wine and handed it to Sasha so she could pour them each a glass while she unpacked the cheese and bread she had brought for them.

Sasha handed her a glass, and with a smile, they touched glasses, saluting the beautiful day they were sharing.

"Please tell me it is always this beautiful," Sasha said as she leaned against the tree.

Milly laughed quietly. "For the next few months it should remain nice, but the winter months can be brutal and

seem to last an eternity with days of endless snow or rain."
Milly looked deep into Sasha's lavender eyes and
continued. "The winds coming in off the river can be bitter,
slicing directly to the bone with its deadly chill."

Sasha could feel warmth pass through Milly's eyes and
into her body as their gaze remained locked. She felt her
cheeks blush from the intense stare of the other woman's
deep blue eyes. The corners of her mouth curled upward in
a small smile and then Milly looked away to begin slicing
the cheese, handing Sasha a large portion with a small loaf
of the crusty bread. They nibbled their lunch and sipped the
sweet red wine while they watched a pair of squirrels
foraging for treasured nuts and acorns to carry into their
nest in preparation for the winter to come.

Sasha was unaccustomed to drinking alcohol and felt a
giddy rush as she sipped the sweet wine.

Milly set down her wineglass and took Sasha's right
hand between hers. "You have the most beautiful hands,"
she said as her fingertips stroked Sasha's skin. "I must
admit I was completely entranced by them as they moved
across the piano keys yesterday."

"Why thank you," Sasha stammered as the now
familiar stirring began deep inside her. She could feel her
heart racing wildly in her chest and hoped Milly would
continue to touch her so sweetly.

Milly eyed the pulse throbbing in Sasha's neck and
could hear the blood as it rushed through her veins,
propelled by her racing heart. She knew from Sasha's
thoughts and her body's response that she was enjoying her
touch. Milly's eyes continued their ascent of Sasha's body.
She noted the slight tremble of Sasha's lips and her smile
broadened when she reached Sasha's eyes to find her
watching her closely.

Milly lifted her right hand to Sasha's face and her
fingers caressed the strong line down her jaw and across her

chin. "You have such strong features. I would love to paint you while you play the piano," she said as she brushed a fingertip across Sasha's lip. "Would you consider sitting for me?"

Sasha had closed her eyes, savoring the rapturous feeling of Milly's touch. Barely registering Milly had asked a question, she asked, "What would you like?"

"I would like you to pose for a painting while you play the piano," Milly repeated. "Would you consider doing that for me?"

"Oh yes," Sasha replied as Milly's fingers drifted across her face with sensual strokes.

It took tremendous restraint from Milly to stop herself from leaning down and kissing the soft lips that begged for a kiss. She wanted their first kiss to be perfect, and she intentionally provoked Sasha's anticipation, as both women knew that soon they would be lovers.

A dark cloud crossed in front of the sun and the wind began to rise. A storm was imminent. The women scrambled to their feet to collect the picnic supplies and rush back toward the carriage. Their perfect moment together was gone as quickly as the sun, now completely concealed by heavy dark clouds. The wind had a chill to it and Milly saw Sasha shiver as she sat close beside her. She reached behind them and draped the picnic quilt around Sasha's shoulders as they headed back to the Jolly Saint Ermins. Milly had pulled underneath the canopy at the front of the hotel just as the heavens exploded with lightning and the clouds dumped a heavy rain on the city.

Both women vibrated with excitement as they ran for cover inside the hotel while a footman cared for the carriage. Sasha led Milly up the stairway to her room and opened the door for her new friend. They would spend the remainder of the afternoon talking while waiting for the storm to pass. Sasha sat on the edge of her bed, the oil flame in the lamp, dimmed during the savagery of the weather, casting a soft shadow on her face. Milly sat at the small desk until an extremely close strike of lightning and an ear-shattering crash of thunder sent them rushing into one another's arms.

Milly again took Sasha's face in her hands, marveling at her beauty and this time could not restrain her desire when she witnessed the pleading look in Sasha's eyes. She bent forward and closed her eyes as her lips encountered Sasha's, and they shared their first tender kiss. Milly's tongue traced the outlines of Sasha's lips, and when she parted them, her tongue disappeared inside Sasha's mouth.

The kiss was Sasha's first truly passionate kiss and her body exploded with sensation as she responded to Milly with a fire of her own. Their tongues swirled together in a sea of arousal. The intensity of emotion made Sasha feel faint and sensing her need, Milly embraced her body for support and led her back over to the bed where she gently laid her down. Milly sat beside her on the bed and held her hand as they searched one another's eyes for reactions to what had just occurred between them.

"That felt fantastic," Sasha finally said as she pulled Milly down on the bed beside her.

Milly answered her by kissing her again as the wind and rain pummeled the window of her room. They shared tender kisses until they realized that the storm had passed and nightfall had arrived. Sasha clung to Milly, not wanting to end their time together.

Milly sensed her anxiety and said, "There will be many more opportunities for us, I promise, but tomorrow you will begin classes as will I, and we both should be well rested."

Milly began to rise off the bed but Sasha pulled her down for a kiss. "When will I see you again?" she asked.

"I will meet you for dinner here tomorrow after classes," Milly said to a smiling Sasha, who stood to walk her to the door.

They shared one final deep kiss before Milly slipped out the door and down the stairway. Sasha rushed to the window to watch as Milly's carriage arrived at the front of the hotel and she climbed into the driver's seat. Milly turned to look up at Sasha's window and saw her standing there. She smiled and waved to Sasha who waved back and then watched as Milly disappeared into the night.

Besieged by a storm of new emotions, Sasha found herself too excited to eat so she quietly undressed and sank into the soft mattress and into dreams of Milly and her sweet kisses.

Milly, too, was alive with excitement as she entered her flat. The day had been wonderful for her as well, and after sketching her memory of Sasha sitting next to the tree, Milly climbed into her bed for a night of rest. Before closing her eyes to slumber, Milly sank into Sasha's dreams and watched as they shared their first kiss again. Smiling peacefully, Milly closed her eyes and allowed sleep to overtake her.

Chapter Six

As Love Grows

Over the next month, Milly and Sasha spent a growing amount of time together. They would see one another briefly on campus, and several nights a week they would meet at Milly's flat for dinner. During these quiet evenings, Sasha sat quietly for Milly as she sketched her portrait as promised. Sasha would practice her lessons and would glance upward to look at Milly as she concentrated on the passion Sasha portrayed while she played the music she loved so dearly. They would attend functions together at the Royal Albert, concerts, and gallery showings of the fine artists that would pass through London on their tour of Europe.

It was during one such evening that Milly put aside her sketchpad and smiled at Sasha. "My darling, would you consider coming to live with me here?" she asked.

Sasha was at first startled by the request. "What would the college think of such an arrangement?"

"It is not all that uncommon that a faculty member invites a foreign student to board in his or her home," Milly answered with a mischievous smile.

Sasha stood and walked toward Milly. "Is that what I would be then, a boarder?" she asked as she circled Milly, her hand running up her right arm, across her shoulders and down her left arm.

Milly clasped Sasha's hand in hers and lowered her to sit on her lap. "Indeed not, I would think," she teased. She

49

reached up, took Sasha's face in her hands, and lowered her face to her lips. The fire behind that kiss left no room for misinterpretation by Sasha that she would be a mere boarder to Milly. When Milly broke the kiss she said, "I selfishly want you near me as much as possible."

"Well, I would be honored to move in with you then, Miss Vansant," Sasha whispered as she leaned in for another kiss.

That kiss lingered as their hands began to explore one another's body. Sasha leaned back and looked deeply into Milly's eyes. "I want to be with you now," Sasha said.

The passion burning in Sasha's eyes left no doubt as to the intent of her words. Milly took her hand and led her to the bedroom. Hands nimbly unfastened the buttons on Sasha's dress and she could hear Sasha's heart race as she lowered the dress from her body. She looked into Sasha's eyes as her fingertips trailed up her arms to slowly lower the straps of her slip and brassiere off her shoulders and down her body. Milly felt Sasha trembling as she caressed the creamy skin left bare to her eyes and touch.

Sasha quivered with anticipation under the touch of Milly's hands as she surrendered her body willingly to the woman who for a month had made love to her in her dreams. Tonight she would experience that love for the first time.

Milly's hands fueled the need in Sasha's body as she removed the remainder of her clothing, and undressed herself before she pressed Sasha backward, placing her on her back on the large bed.

Sasha watched Milly, her eyes shining with passion as Milly lowered her body until their heated skin touched, her nipples dragging slowly across Sasha's skin. Sasha moaned loudly as Milly's body nestled gently between her inflamed thighs, wetness upon wetness. Milly smiled at her and covered her mouth with a passionate kiss as her hips began to undulate against Sasha's body.

Sasha's body burned with a desire so intense it exceeded her dreams as her body responded to every touch and kiss. Milly kissed down her neck, licking the jugular vein that pulsed with each beat of her lover's thundering heart. Sasha's arousal soared as Milly moved down her body, gently lapping at her skin with a soft tongue. Milly's fingertips teased her swollen nipples until Sasha feared she would scream, and she groaned loudly when Milly took a breast in her mouth and began to suckle her.

Milly's right hand moved down between their bodies and stroked through the wetness, tracing Sasha's swollen lips with gentle fingertips as her teeth lightly bit her nipple. She could feel Sasha's body writhing with need, and she parted her lower lips, penetrating her with two fingers. Milly explored the velvety cavern within Sasha with tender fingers that ignited her climax as she withdrew and re-entered Sasha's body, pressing deeper with each stroke. Sasha's hips bucked against Milly's hand as her body exploded and released a flood of juices into Milly's palm.

Milly continued down Sasha's body until her mouth covered her wetness. Her tongue brushed the fingers still buried inside Sasha's body and lapped at the juices flowing from her. As her fingers curled and flexed, Milly's tongue discovered the small button of pleasure that had escaped the protective hood to become prey for her tongue. As she licked across the throbbing bud and sucked it gently into her mouth, Sasha cried out in pleasure, her body thrashing frantically beneath Milly as her body erupted in orgasm again.

Milly remained still inside Sasha until her body began to calm then she slowly withdrew her fingers and climbed back up the bed to cover Sasha's mouth with hers. Sasha tasted her juices in the mouth of her lover and her tongue

51

danced wildly in Milly's mouth as she savored the memory of her first taste.

Sasha was eager to give Milly pleasure in return, and rolled her over onto her back. She mimicked each of Milly's movements on her body, lavishing tender kisses on her breasts. When her fingers entered Milly, Sasha groaned loudly with her lover as the liquid velvet welcomed her probing fingers. She hungered to taste Milly and when her mouth was inches from her swollen lower lips, Sasha breathed deeply of the scent of her lover and then lowered her mouth to drink from her well as Milly's hands played in her hair and guided the movement of her mouth. When Milly reached her climax, she coated Sasha's face with her sweet nectar and greedily lapped it up with her tongue. She could feel the inner muscles of Milly's body convulse around her fingers as the spasms of her orgasm continued for several minutes.

Tears of complete rapture flowed down Sasha's cheeks as she moved up Milly's body to kiss her deeply. Milly embraced Sasha's soul at that moment and held her close for several hours as they enjoyed the comfort of one another's body.

Sasha looked into Milly's eyes, overwhelmed by the intense feeling of contentment she felt in her lover's arms. Never in her most heated dreams had she experienced the arousal that Milly stirred deep in her body. Sasha craved Milly's touch and thirsted for her passionate kisses that brought such a beautiful feeling of rapture to her body.

By the time Sasha left the flat that evening, they decided she would move the following weekend, a mere day away, and she eagerly began packing her belongings. Before retiring for the evening, she wrote her parents a letter explaining the move and providing them her new address. She added several newspaper clippings reviewing her performances at the college concerts and prepared it for posting.

✝

By the end of Saturday, Sasha's belongings had been stored into the small spare bedroom in Milly's flat. This would be a ruse to any visitor they may have as neither woman intended to sleep alone.

Months passed quickly as Sasha and Milly grew deeper in love. Milly would paint for hours in her studio after dinner, and after six months, the portrait of Sasha had been finished and hung above the fireplace. Milly had captured the essence of Sasha so brilliantly in the painting that Sasha sometimes felt she was looking into a mirror. Milly was able to astound Sasha with the beauty of her paintings and the devotion and passion she shared with Sasha in the comforts of their home.

Every few weeks, though, Sasha would wake in the early morning hours to find the bed next to her cold and empty. She would creep from the comfort of the bed and search through the flat to find she was alone before crawling back into the warmth of the bed. She would wake several hours later when Milly returned to their bed, snuggling her chilled body into Sasha's warmth before drifting into sleep.

Sasha never asked Milly where she went so late at night, satisfied that Milly would tell her when she felt she needed to know. Blinded by the love she had for Milly, Sasha knew nothing outside the reaches of their home could make a difference.

Sasha's musical talent continued to improve and she began to receive requests for performances in Christiania, Paris, and other fine venues. She was delighted to perform for the British Cabinet at the Royal Albert during the

Christmas break. Sasha wrote to Theo to inform him of this honor, and, with Milly's blessing, she invited her parents to spend the Christmas holidays with them in London.

†

When Milly and Sasha met Theo and Marie at the train station, Sasha was again surprised at how much her mother had aged during their separation while Theo remained the vision of health with his stunning good looks.

"Mother and Father, I would like to introduce you to Milly Vansant," Sasha said.

"It is such a pleasure to finally meet you, Milly," Marie said. "Sasha has written so much about you."

Theo took Milly's hand in his and bent forward to kiss it softly. "Thank you for inviting us to share the holidays with you."

"It is my pleasure to have you both as guests," Milly said.

Theo was quick to deduce why Sasha had written so fondly of Milly as he watched the two women interact. His daughter was deeply in love, though publicly their behavior was proper toward one another. Theo knew his daughter was happy and had found her mate. His only fear was that Sasha would be so in love that she would never return to the States, but even that would be a small sacrifice for his daughter's happiness.

†

On Christmas Day, Theo saw the portrait of Sasha that Milly had painted for the first time. He knew then that Milly saw Sasha in a special light. As they waited for the traditional Christmas feast that Milly was preparing, Theo found himself glancing up at the portrait often.

†

54

"That was a fantastic meal," Theo said later as he pushed the plate from his reach.

"I am glad you enjoyed it and I hope you saved room for dessert," Milly said.

"My goodness no, Milly, I am so stuffed I couldn't eat another bite right now," Theo said.

"Very well, we will retire to the living room for a cup of tea and allow your meal to settle. I would bet that within an hour your stomach will be ready for some of my special bread pudding."

"Is it drizzled with whiskey sauce?" Theo asked.

"It most certainly is," Milly said with a warm smile.

Theo sat beside Marie on a love seat and looked at his beautiful wife. "How would you like to move to London?" he teased.

"Milly dear, I think you are spoiling my husband," Marie said with a chuckle.

"How can that be, Mother, since he is already spoiled rotten," Sasha teased as she ruffled her father's hair.

Theo looked around the room at the three women. "I am surrounded and outnumbered," he cried out.

Sasha and Milly broke out with laughter at Theo's dramatics.

The kettle whistled and Milly stood to go to the kitchen to prepare their tea. "Would you like some help, Milly?" Marie asked.

"I would love some," she answered.

When they had left the room, Sasha looked at Theo. "So what do you think?"

"Think about what?" Theo said coyly.

"Tell me what you think about Milly, Father," Sasha pleaded.

"I think she is beautiful and warmhearted," Theo said. "I also think she has stolen my daughter's heart."

"Yes, Father, she has. I love her so," Sasha said.

"She is a great cook, too, and I can't wait to sample her bread pudding," Theo said with a grin.

"You are so predictable, Father," Sasha said with a laugh.

Theo watched Sasha's face light up as Milly and Marie returned with their tea. He smiled at the gentle touches and loving looks they gave one another as they drank their tea.

Milly filled Theo's belly with bread pudding and sent a small container back to the hotel with him later in the evening.

✝

Theo and Marie spent nearly two weeks in London with Sasha and Milly and were extremely proud of the performance Sasha gave at the hall.

The day before her parents were to return home, Milly woke Sasha with a sweet kiss. "I have a question for you," she said to a still sleepy Sasha.

"What is it, my love?" Sasha asked.

"Would you mind if we gave your father the portrait of you?" she asked.

Sasha looked at her curiously. "I know he misses you terribly and he was so drawn to the portrait. I think we should give it to him," Milly added.

"I think that would be a kind gesture," Sasha said as she embraced her love. "Father will put up an argument, but I know he would love to have the painting."

"Fine, it is settled then. Tonight when they come for dinner we will present it to him," Milly said.

When they finally crept from the warmth of their bed, they found it was snowing outside. Sasha dressed warmly and left the flat to meet her father for a walk. Confined to the ship's limited deck space for five days Theo would enjoy a walk with her. Her steps crunched in the fresh, crisp snow as she rushed to find Theo.

†

Theo was waiting for Sasha under the canopy when she arrived and they began their stroll. Sasha took care in pointing out areas of special interest to him and it was evident to Theo that his daughter was happy in London.

"It is so good to see you happy again," Theo said as they walked. "You vibrate with the excitement of life."

"I love this city and the college and the many opportunities I have been afforded here," Sasha said.

"Do you know what your plans will be once you graduate?" Theo asked.

"I would like to spend another year in Europe performing, and after that I am not sure."

"Do you think you and Milly will be coming back to the States?" her father asked.

Sasha was pleased that her father saw Milly as someone significant in her future. "We have not discussed the future, Father, but yes, I could see us living in New Orleans, or maybe even New York."

"You know you both would be welcome in our home, if you choose New Orleans," Theo said.

"Thank you, Father, your acceptance means everything to me and to us," Sasha said, speaking on Milly's behalf. Theo's unspoken acceptance of her chosen lifestyle was a great relief to Sasha, and she took her father's arm as they walked on.

"We will gladly welcome another daughter into the family," he said.

"That is very sweet of you to say, and I know Milly thinks highly of you and Mother," Sasha said.

Theo and Sasha continued their stroll as the snowflakes grew larger.

"Will you come to visit again when I graduate, Father?" Sasha asked.

"That is a silly question, you should know that Mother and I would not miss such a milestone in your life," Theo said. "Of course we will be here."

They walked for nearly another hour before returning to the hotel. Theo and Sasha parted with a promise to meet at five for dinner at Milly's flat. Sasha left her father and walked home, oblivious to the snowflakes that were falling faster and growing larger by the hour.

†

Marie and Theo arrived promptly at five, just as Milly and Sasha were setting the table. The smell of fresh-baked bread lingered in the air as Milly placed several small loaves on the table to cool.

Sasha poured glasses of wine and joined her parents and Milly in the small room housing the fireplace. Sasha caught her father glancing at the vacant spot where her portrait had hung and prompted Milly by saying, "I do believe Milly has a parting gift for you, Father."

Theo looked at Milly, who was grinning from ear to ear, and opened his mouth to protest. "I will not take no for an answer, so you may as well save your breath," Milly teased. "Sasha and I have decided to give you her portrait to take back to New Orleans." She slid the heavily wrapped framed portrait over to Theo.

Theo began to stutter. "Just say thank you, Theo," Marie said to her husband.

Theo was shocked at the gift and after several seconds of stunned silence was indeed able to thank Milly and Sasha for their gift. Theo spent the rest of the evening grinning widely and carefully tucked his treasure under his arm when they stood to return to the hotel.

"We will meet you in the morning," Sasha said as they walked to the door together. She opened the door to see the ground covered with white powder, but the snow had stopped falling. "Be careful, Father. I know you do not see too much snow in New Orleans and walking in it can sometimes be tricky," she said just as Theo stepped onto a frozen patch and slid a few inches.

Theo laughed and shouted back, "Do not curse me, Daughter," as he clutched tighter at his portrait.

Milly and Sasha watched them until they disappeared into the night and then returned inside to snuggle on the couch in front of the fire. Sasha saw Milly glance up at the blank space where the portrait had hung. "Thank you for your generosity to my father," she said. "He adores that painting, you know."

"The painting was good, but I will be satisfied with the live subject," Milly said with a soft kiss to Sasha's cheek.

"Will you?" Sasha asked with an impish tone in her voice as she leaned closer to Milly.

"Most definitely." Milly embraced Sasha for a deep, passionate kiss. "Why don't we move to the bedroom where I can show you how satisfied I can be," Milly taunted her lover.

Milly led Sasha to the bedroom and slowly undressed her lover, covering her skin with burning kisses as she lowered Sasha's clothing and eased her back on the bed. Milly and Sasha kissed and caressed one another deep into the night until with a heavy sigh Milly said, "You leave me entirely satisfied, lover."

With a smile and a final kiss, the lovers rested for the remainder of the night, arms and legs entwined in a sensual embrace.

†

The following morning, they met Theo and Marie at the hotel and walked with them to the train station. Sasha and Milly had agreed the previous night that they would take the train to Liverpool with Theo and Marie to see them board the ship.

During the train ride, Theo talked excitedly about his business and Sasha could tell her father was longing for home.

"Thank you both so much for allowing us to share the holidays with you," Theo said when the train pulled into the station.

"It was a pleasure to meet you both, and I hope to see you again when Sasha graduates," Milly said.

"You most definitely will," Theo said as he offered his arm to Marie and they left the train.

Milly and Sasha both received warm embraces from Theo and Marie and then stood together waving as the ship left the harbor for the return journey to the States. Sasha shed quiet tears in Milly's arms, saddened by the departure of her parents.

Chapter Seven

The Truth

It would be another year and a half before Theo and Marie returned to London for Sasha's graduation. During this time, Sasha and Milly's love for one another continued to grow until they were nearly inseparable.

In the early spring, before her graduation, Sasha's curiosity finally got the best of her. She and Milly had been lovers for almost two years, but Sasha knew there was a part of Milly that she kept hidden from her. One evening, when Sasha woke again to find she was alone in their bed, she made up her mind to ask Milly where she went when she disappeared in the middle of the night. Sitting up in the middle of the bed with the covers pulled up around her shoulders, she forced herself to remain awake until Milly returned. Her heart raced in her chest as her imagination ran wild, thinking of what Milly's answer could be. She knew her lover was different from others, but they had never spent much time discussing Milly's past.

Sasha was startled when she heard the doorknob turn and the door opened. She could hear the soft footsteps as Milly approached the bedroom. Milly sensed that Sasha was awake and paused before she entered the room. She could feel Sasha's anxiety as she entered her thoughts, and she knew the answers to the questions Sasha was preparing to ask would change their lives forever. Bolstering her courage, Milly stepped into the bedroom.

"Did I wake you, my love?" she asked innocently.

"I woke to find the bed empty and I started to worry," Sasha said. "I noticed that this occurs every few weeks and I realized I have no idea of where you go or what you are doing while you are gone."

Milly walked to the bed as Sasha's worried frown continued to grow and sat next to her lover. "The time has come for us to discuss my past and our future," Milly said as she forced a smile to her face. There was no doubt that Sasha loved her, she was confident of that, but would their love be strong enough to endure the truth Milly was about to share with her? Milly prayed that it would as she reached for Sasha's hand.

"What I am about to tell you, you may not believe, but my words are spoken truly."

Sasha searched Milly's eyes. There was a feral look behind them and she knew her lover was afraid, but of what she had no idea.

"I hope you know that my love for you is sincere and that I want to spend eternity with you," Milly said.

"I love you too," Sasha said as she smiled sweetly. "I realized tonight as I lay awake waiting for your return that I know very little about you, Milly, and you have hidden part of your life from me."

"I have," Milly said. "You must trust me and listen carefully to what I am about to reveal to you, because what I will tell you will shock you to your core and may repulse you so badly you may wish to never see me again."

Sasha watched as the tears welled up in Milly's eyes and she reached out to caress her lover's cheek. "Tell me then," she softly said.

"I am not who you believe me to be," Milly said. "Yes, my name and occupation are correct, but I am not a thirty-year-old woman as you believe."

Sasha's confusion contorted her face as she struggled to understand.

"I was born in eighteen hundred and ten," Milly said.

"That's impossible," Sasha said. "That would make you over a hundred, and you are young and beautiful."

"It is the truth, Sasha," Milly said. "When I was in my early twenties, I was studying in France and I became involved with one of my tutors." She paused. "Anne was a beautiful young woman who was a gifted artist, and she shared one of her gifts with me." Milly braced herself and continued. "Anne was blessed with the gift of immortality and cursed by the need to drink human blood to maintain her existence."

Milly could feel Sasha stiffen as she spoke these words. "You mean she was a vampire?" Sasha asked. "I thought vampires were mythical creatures that lured their prey to their deaths by their erotic temptations."

"Quite the contrary," Milly said. "Vampires are real and not the fictional characters of horrific tales to keep unruly children at bay as once supposed."

Sasha's eyes grew wide when the realization of Milly's words began to sink into her. She withdrew her hand from Milly's and moved back to sit against the headboard with her arms protectively wrapped around her raised knees. "So when you disappear at night?" she asked.

"When I disappear at night, I hunt. The curse of being a vampire is that I must feed on human blood to maintain my existence."

"So you willingly go out and murder someone?" Sasha asked.

Milly blanched at Sasha's use of the word murder, but in fact, she was correct. "To keep myself alive, yes, I do," she answered. "I will not attempt to justify that fact, but I do hunt for those that are dying already or someone who is so vile that the world would be better off in their absence."

"So does this mean you are dead?" Sasha asked.

"Not in the sense that you would use to describe death," Milly said. She struggled for a moment until she found the correct words to describe her life. "I died as a human to be reborn as an immortal," she said. "But as you have witnessed yourself, I eat, drink, breathe, hurt, and experience joy and love just as you, with one major difference."

"What is the one major difference?" Sasha asked.

"That if I hunt responsibly and remain vigilant of my surroundings, I will live for hundreds of years," Milly said.

Sasha's head was spinning. The information Milly was sharing with her left her dazed and confused. "How do you live in the daytime?" Sasha asked. "I thought daylight was deadly to vampires, but you do not appear affected by it in the least."

"I was fortunate to be reborn as a day walker," Milly said. "As with human evolution, mutations have occurred in the vampire world which allows us to adapt to the world as it changes. To appear normal to the outside world, we have to blend into their society to survive."

Milly was surprised when Sasha did not act terrified by what she was telling her. Startled yes, but not horrified. Her curiosity burned as hundreds of questions formed in her head. She relaxed on the bed and asked her next question. "You can read my mind, can't you?"

"I have the ability to enter your thoughts to determine what you are thinking, yes," Milly answered honestly. "I can see what you are thinking and experience how you feel, but I do not project into your thoughts."

"But you could if you wanted to?" Sasha asked.

"Yes, I could project suggestions into your thoughts, but I would never do this without your permission."

"Do it now," Sasha said.

Milly fixed Sasha with her deep blue eyes. *Kiss me* was the thought she projected to her.

Sasha smiled, leaned forward, and planted a kiss on Milly's lips without a second thought. When she again sat up in the bed, she had a puzzled look on her face. "So you could be controlling me and I would never know any different?" she asked.

"I could, yes, but I have not been," Milly said, somewhat hurt by Sasha's accusation. "I love you deeply and would never attempt to control you, Sasha."

Sasha sensed Milly's despair. "I didn't think you would, darling." Sasha remained silent for a few minutes and then asked her next question. "What happened to Anne?"

"We lived together for almost ten years in different parts of Europe. One night she was careless in her hunting and the authorities became aware of her patterns and lay in wait for her next hunting trip."

Sasha could sense the loss and sadness Milly felt as she continued. "They set a trap and Anne had become complacent due to her abilities. She was ambushed and destroyed by her attackers," Milly said, a shiver running down her spine. "In her last moments, Anne projected to me and warned me of the impending danger, which allowed me to escape before I too could be hunted down."

"You loved her," Sasha said, more of a statement than a question.

"Yes, I did, but I fled the city that night knowing she was lost to me forever and have changed locations often since then to prevent detection."

"Have you been alone this entire time?" Sasha asked.

Milly nodded. "The loneliness was unbearable at times, but I was not comfortable sharing my true self with anyone until you. When I saw you that day at the piano, your fingers stroked my heart with the same gentleness they did the keys, and I knew I must be with you, even if only for a short time."

Sasha looked toward the window to find that the sun had risen and felt a great desire to be outside as she digested this new information. She stood up and began to dress. "I need to think for a while," she said and, after a soft kiss, walked past Milly and out the door.

Milly watched as Sasha left the flat. She feared her revelation would cause her to leave and never return. She could only wait and hope that Sasha's love would lead her back.

†

Sasha wandered the streets of London for hours, walking aimlessly, her head still spinning from her conversation with Milly. The loneliness in her voice as she talked about Anne struck Sasha's heart deeply. She understood the sadness of losing someone she dearly loved, but she could not fathom carrying that memory alone for so many years. Sasha had no doubts about her love for Milly, but for a moment, she wished she had not insisted on knowing who Milly really was.

Could she come to terms with what Milly was? she asked herself as she walked.

It had taken great courage for Milly to tell her the truth and Sasha would not rush into judgment of her. She had shown her nothing but kindness and love since they met, and Sasha had given thought to growing old with Milly. Now she realized that this could never be, for as an immortal Milly would not grow old for centuries.

Sasha's feet led her to the spot where she and Milly had picnicked under the large old tree. She sat and leaned against it the way she had that day and gazed into the sky. So much had passed between them since that day, and she found herself smiling as she thought of Milly. Sasha remembered the way her love for Amelia had felt betrayed and vowed she would not allow that to happen to Milly. She was not certain what their future would be, but for now Sasha would be content. Tears of happiness slid down her cheeks and the sky opened up to shed tears of its own as a spring shower began to fall.

Sasha was soaked to the bone when she returned to the flat. Milly was preparing soup for their dinner and rushed across the room when she entered.

"You will catch your death of cold, if you stand there in these wet clothes," she scolded.

Milly reached to unbutton her dress but Sasha caught up her hands, bringing them to her mouth and kissing each one of them. "I love you and that is all that matters."

Milly embraced Sasha, oblivious to the soaked clothing, and their lips melted together in a passionate kiss. Milly's hands worked the fasteners free, slid the damp clothing down her lover's body, and led her to the bed. Her own clothing disappeared quickly and she joined Sasha under the covers, warming her lover's body with heated kisses as her fingers ignited their most primal passions. The intensity of their lovemaking lasted for hours, until finally sated they lay panting in each other's arms.

"So much for the soup," Sasha said with a laugh.

"It has probably been scorched beyond hope," Milly said, returning her smile. Milly climbed from the bed and walked into the kitchen. Checking the soup, she found it still edible, portioned out a large bowl of it, along with fresh bread and cheese, and carried it to the bedroom.

They feasted together on the bed and then entwined their bodies under the warmth of the blankets and slipped into a blissful sleep.

Chapter Eight

Paris

Graduation day arrived, and when Theo and Marie left London for the second time, they begged Sasha and Milly to come home with them. Theo was worried about the rumblings of a possible war and the safety of his daughter in these parts, full of volatile and aggressive leaders.

As they walked to the harbor in Liverpool, Theo draped his arm around Sasha's shoulder and said, "Please heed my warnings and come home if this terrible war does begin."

"We will be careful, Father," Sasha said. "If it becomes too dangerous, we will come home, I promise."

Disappointed that he could not persuade the two women to leave Europe with them, Theo and Marie boarded the ship and sailed for home.

†

Milly and Sasha stood at the pier railing to watch them board the ship. "You know your father may be correct in his assumptions," Milly said. "Rumors abound in regard to the unrest of several nations, and it is unlikely that England would refrain from joining the war if her borders are threatened."

"If, and when that time does come, will you come to America with me?" Sasha asked.

"Yes, I will, my love," Milly answered.

They watched the ship sail from the harbor and then walked back to the train station for the now familiar ride to London. Once back inside their flat, Sasha took Milly in her arms and kissed her deeply, leaving her lover breathless.

"What was that for?" Milly asked innocently.

"Just for being my love," Sasha answered. "You know I will be leaving for Paris in a few weeks for a series of concerts, and I was hoping you would join me," she said.

"A few weeks in Paris with a beautiful young woman, how could I resist?" Milly teased. "Yes, I will join you. I have no intention of setting you free in such a romantic city all alone."

Sasha kissed the tip of her nose. "I was hoping you would travel with me. Maybe you can give me a personal tour of the city," Sasha said as she pulled Milly to her again.

"For kisses like yours, I would follow you anywhere."

†

The weeks passed quickly and Milly and Sasha arrived in Paris under a sky full of bright stars. After checking into the hotel, they sat out on their private balcony for hours gazing at the skies and enjoying one another's company. The next day, Sasha located the concert hall and arranged to practice for several hours later in the day. She would perform twice each week for two weeks before returning to London, so she and Milly had plenty of time to explore the great city.

On the night before her final performance, she and Milly walked through the vast public gardens. Flowers scented the air as they strolled and Sasha took Milly's hand in hers. They walked until they found a bench. Sitting beside the river, they looked across it to the wondrous view of the city in lights.

"I have been thinking," Sasha said. She turned on the bench to face Milly, who was watching her closely. "I have decided that I want to be with you forever."

"Forever is a long time, my love," Milly said as she took Sasha's chin in her hand. "There is no rush, so you need to take your time and be certain of your decision. This life is difficult and you need to be sure you can watch those you love grow old and die, while you age ever so slowly."

"I have been thinking about this for months," Sasha said. "I know I want to be with you forever, at any cost."

Milly's eyes searched Sasha's face as she tried to conceal her excitement at Sasha's revelation. She saw no hesitation in Sasha's expression and sighed. "The physical pain will be intense, but will last for just a few hours if we are fortunate," Milly explained. "Will you be able to deal with the need to feed on human blood?"

"I am sure I will feel some guilt over taking another life, at first, but if that is what it takes to be with you, I will deal with it," Sasha said.

"You will have no choice once you are reborn, Sasha," Milly said. "You need to know what the hunt will be like."

"So take me with you," Sasha said.

Milly looked deep into Sasha's eyes "Is that really what you want?"

"I think it is important if I need to know," Sasha boldly said, her eyes staring back at Milly.

"Very well then, tomorrow night after your performance, we will hunt." Milly sat back against the bench, unsure if Sasha was aware of what she was asking. If the trauma was too intense for her, Milly could erase that memory for Sasha and she would be none the wiser.

†

The following evening, Sasha performed her final concert in Paris and her lavender eyes were alight with the excitement of performing as she took her final applause and left the stage. Milly was proudly waiting at the end of the stage for her lover. "That was a beautiful performance, my love," she said as she embraced Sasha.

"Thank you, Milly. It makes it even more special to know you are in the audience," she said as she returned the embrace. "Let's make a polite appearance and then escape this place," Sasha whispered in Milly's ear.

Milly smiled and nodded her agreement to Sasha's suggestion. She could feel the arousal coursing through Sasha and knew her lover needed her special attention. Milly was eager to attend to Sasha's needs and once the required appearance was made, she and Sasha slipped into the Paris night.

Back at the hotel Milly assisted Sasha in removing her performance dress and hung it in the closet, leaving her in thin undergarments as she removed her own clothing. Sasha watched her every movement with hungry eyes, and Milly decided to take her lover slowly, intensifying the growing need. They lay back onto the bed and Milly began covering Sasha with tender kisses. Sasha's skin burned for Milly's touch as her hands explored Sasha's body. Her fingertips moved beneath the thin undergarments to softly stroke the sensitive flesh as Sasha's breath caught in her throat. Her tender caresses continued until Sasha arched her back, offering her body to Milly as her eyes begged for release.

Sasha removed the camisole and Milly's fingers disappeared between her quaking thighs as her mouth enclosed Sasha's breast and she began to suckle. She positioned her body above Sasha to allow Sasha's fingers to explore her wetness. Sasha did not hesitate at the invitation and plunged her fingers into the welcoming wetness as Milly began nibbling her nipple and thrusting deeply inside her. Both were lost in the frenzy of arousal as their bodies coiled and exploded in violent climaxes repeatedly until the lovers were exhausted and their need sated.

Milly pulled the covers over their bodies and cradled Sasha in sleep for several hours. Milly then softly kissed her lover awake. "It is time to hunt," she whispered.

†

They dressed, and Milly could see the excitement glowing in Sasha's eyes as they walked out to the dimly lit streets. Milly knew from experience that this time of morning would be perfect for prey that would be out stalking victims of his or her own. They passed pubs and brothels hidden by dark alleys and Milly's mind reached out in search of prey.

Milly took Sasha's hand and led her to the back of one of the darkest alleys. Milly held Sasha's hand and said, "I will open my mind to you and you will witness what I see and feel."

Sasha nodded her head in acknowledgment. Milly's mind entered the small apartment backing onto the alley, and they could only watch as a man brutally took his pleasure from the young woman, barely more than a child, who was pinned beneath his slovenly body. The haunting whimpers from the woman as the man degraded her body would ring in Milly's ears until she drank the last drop of blood from his vile body. She watched as the man finished and with a disgusting leer dropped two small pieces of silver next to the woman. "Hardly worth the effort," the man growled as he fastened his pants and left the apartment. Sasha felt complete disgust for the vile man, and felt a seething hatred pulse through her veins as he abused the young woman.

"Wait here," Milly said to Sasha, and she stepped into the faint light as the man approached.

Sasha leaned next to a tree to conceal her presence and felt Milly enter her mind. She could feel the anger and excitement racing through her lover's body as she stalked her prey.

"Well, aren't you a tasty morsel," the man said as Milly continued to walk toward him. "How much?" he asked.

"Free for you," Milly said as she led him from under the light and into a darker corner.

Sasha watched as Milly pushed the man into the wall with a surprising strength, knocking the breath from him shortly.

"You like it rough, do you?" the man breathed heavily.

Milly placed her hands on the large man's shoulders and forced him to his knees. Sasha watched as Milly's fangs grew and were now exposed to the man, whose eyes were wide with terror, his muscles paralyzed by his fear. Milly lowered her head and Sasha felt the plunge of fangs into the man's neck as Milly began to drink. Sasha could taste the salty mixture of the man's blood as it pulsed from his body with each beat of his wildly racing heart. Sasha's vision swirled with red and white waves of light as she felt the pleasure Milly felt while she feasted on the man. She listened as his heartbeat grew faint, and then completely extinguished as Milly took his life.

Sasha felt her knees weaken and then buckle as the intense emotions she had felt from Milly left her drained of strength.

Disgusted by the vile man, Milly sealed the wounds and then discarded his body in a remote wooded area behind the alley. She then took the man's purse, filled with gold and silver coins, and placed it on the young prostitute's doorstep. She knocked on the door and retreated to the seclusion of the trees with Sasha, who had struggled back to her feet. They watched as the young woman, still crying from her encounter with the man, discovered the purse, and after looking around in the darkness, slipped quietly back inside her apartment.

Milly and Sasha walked, talking about the encounter until the sun came up and then returned to the hotel for a few hours' sleep, before their scheduled departure for London. As Milly wrapped Sasha in her arms she asked, "Do you still want to join me?"

"Yes, more than ever," Sasha said, and with a final kiss, she snuggled deeper into Milly's arms and drifted off into sleep.

Chapter Nine

Reborn

Sasha had requested Milly transform her on her coming birthday, and as the day approached their excitement grew. They had both been busy with arranging concert tours and gallery showings since their return to London, but they had agreed they would remain at home during July to allow Sasha time to adjust to her new life.

When the day finally arrived, Milly spent most of it describing to Sasha what she would experience during her rebirth and then afterward when she awoke as an immortal. Sasha listened intently to every word and asked questions when she did not understand.

"I will take your life from you by draining your body of its life force of blood. You will feel very little while this occurs, but your body will fight against it in its struggle to survive," Milly explained as she stroked Sasha's hair. "As the life fades from your body, you will relax and there will be nothing but absolute blackness for a time." Milly looked into her eyes and said, "Each rebirth is different, but I am telling you what I know will occur from my experience and the rest we will have to take as it comes."

"I know I will be safe with you," Sasha said.

Milly smiled at the confidence Sasha had in her, and continued. "Once your human life has vanished, I will open a vein in my wrist and you will drink from my body," Milly said. "You will be tempted to drink deeply as my blood will quench the fire in your body, but you will be given only what you need. As my blood nourishes your body, you will be reborn and your heart will once more start to beat, getting stronger with each mouthful."

Sasha looked at her with complete adoration in her eyes.

Milly's hand caressed Sasha's face. "You will not be able to see, or speak, or hear at this point, but I will remain beside you until your birth is complete," Milly promised. "Your body will be wracked with agonizing pain as it physically transforms from human to immortal and you will relive my entire life, all the pain, trauma, and the happy times in hours." She sighed deeply. "It will almost be like the pages of a book being fanned in front of your eyes, years passing in mere minutes."

Sasha listened intently. "When the birth is complete and your body is exhausted by the transformation, you will sleep for a time. When you wake again, you will have begun your new life as an immortal." Milly kissed Sasha softly. "You will feel weak for a few days and it may take weeks to adjust to your heightened senses, but adjust you will," she promised. "Then we will hunt and you will feed on your first human, something you will need to do every few weeks."

"How will I know?" Sasha asked.

"Your body will let you know when it is time to hunt and your instincts will take over." Milly reached over to touch Sasha's stomach. "A fire will burn here that can only be quenched by human blood and it will continue to grow to the point of near madness until you feed."

Milly went to the kitchen and poured them each a glass of wine. Taking Sasha's hand, she led her into the bedroom. They sat on the bed and drank the wine and then Milly asked, "Are you absolutely certain Sasha that this life is what you want? There is still time to change your mind, but once we begin, there is no turning back."

"Without a doubt," Sasha answered.

Milly stood and took the empty glasses to the kitchen and returned to undress Sasha completely, laying her naked body upon soft linens. Milly lay down next to her and kissed her deeply. "Relax and close your eyes, my love, and when you awaken we will be together forever," Milly promised.

"I love you," Sasha whispered.

"I love you too," Milly said as she took Sasha in her arms and gently brushed the hair from around her neck. She could see Sasha's pulse dancing wildly as she lowered her head to sink her fangs into the soft tissue of Sasha's neck.

Sasha felt the initial pain as Milly's fangs sank into her flesh and then felt nothing. Her body convulsed briefly as Milly drank from her until her body, drained of blood, resigned itself to death.

After the final heartbeat, Milly raised her mouth from Sasha's neck, then cradling her in her arms she bit her own wrist and opened a vein, the blood flowing freely in her excited state. Milly held the limp, lifeless body of her lover in her arms and marveled that even in death her beauty remained. Milly placed her opened vein to Sasha's mouth and whispered "Drink" in a soft command.

Sasha slowly returned to life as Milly's blood flowed into her body. Her lips began to move as the blood trickled past her lips and she drank in Milly's offering. Milly listened carefully for the return of a heartbeat and smiled when she heard the gentle thumping begin in Sasha's chest. The beat grew stronger, and when Milly saw the wound in Sasha's neck heal itself, she removed her wrist from Sasha's mouth and laid her body back on the bed.

Sasha felt cold and terrified in the complete darkness. She struggled to move her paralyzed body and then the memory of Milly's words flooded her brain. "Relax and close your eyes, and when you awaken, we will be together forever." She stopped struggling and slipped further into the darkness.

The darkness overtook her and Sasha's body began to convulse. Milly stayed beside her for hours, bathing her heated body with cool cloths to comfort her love during her transition. Milly had begun to worry when finally, in the early hours of the morning, Sasha gasped for a deep breath, the convulsions finally stopped, and she slept peacefully.

Milly lay beside her and covered Sasha's body with the soft bed linens. She watched her sleep for hours and then decided to rest herself for a while.

†

Hours later, Milly awoke to the feel of Sasha snuggling into her body and she knew it wouldn't be much longer before her lover awoke. She held Sasha close and waited until her eyes began to flutter. "Welcome, my love," she whispered.

Sasha smiled, but could not yet form speech. She laid her head on Milly's shoulder and napped for the remainder of the day.

Milly had slipped from the bed while Sasha rested and had returned to sit beside the bed. Watching Sasha sleep so peacefully, Milly's head began to nod and when she woke, she felt Sasha's eyes on her. She looked up to find Sasha smiling at her.

"Wouldn't you be more comfortable over here?" she asked weakly as she patted the bed beside her.

"Yes, I would." Milly crawled into bed next to her lover. "How are you feeling?" she asked.

"Like I have been torn apart and sewn back together with a few extra pieces," Sasha weakly answered.

"Well, that is not too far from what your body experienced," Milly said. "The extra pieces are your senses that have been fine-tuned to be hypersensitive. For instance, can you hear my heartbeat?"

Sasha closed her eyes and listened and she could indeed hear the thudding beat of Milly's heart.

"Yes, I can," Sasha said with a smile.

"Can you taste the sweetness of the rain that has fallen outside for the last few hours?" she asked.

"Yes, and I can hear the chattering of the little mouse in the kitchen that you have been secretly feeding for weeks now," Sasha said with a grin.

"Good, now that you are awake, we will practice some of your other skills," Milly said. "For the remainder of the day, you will not speak to me to let me know your needs; you will use your mind to project them to me, agreed?"

"Agreed," Sasha said aloud. She held back a chuckle as Milly scolded her for speaking. *Kiss me then, my love,* she projected.

"Good," Milly said and rewarded her with a sweet kiss.

I am thirsty. May I have a glass of water?

Milly went to the kitchen to pour a glass of water for her. She could feel Sasha expanding her range as her mind began to tickle. *Feed your pet while you are in there, he's hungry,* Sasha projected.

Milly laughed and said, "I see that you are a quick learner, my love." She walked back into the bedroom. "One of the most difficult tasks will be controlling the sound of all the heartbeats and blood rushing when you are in a crowd or walking down the street." She handed Sasha the water. "At first, the cacophony of sounds may drive you insane until you learn to control them," she said, "but that is a skill we can work on tomorrow." She watched Sasha drink deeply from the glass. "Rest is what your body needs tonight." She took the glass from her lover and pulled the covers over her body again.

Sasha awoke the next morning to the smell of bacon and fresh biscuits and crept from the bed, pulling a robe around her shoulders. "I am ravenous," she said as she walked into the kitchen.

"Have a seat then, breakfast will be ready soon," Milly said. "I have fresh coffee if you would like."

"That would be wonderful," Sasha said as she smiled weakly.

"How are you feeling this morning?" Milly asked.

"Much better than last night, but as weak as a newborn kitten," Sasha said.

"Some food will help," Milly said as she placed a platter of food in front of her and returned for the coffee mugs. "Eat now, you can rest afterward."

Sasha ate her fill of the breakfast and drank two mugs of coffee before she began to feel sleepy again. Milly led her back to bed and waited until Sasha returned to sleep. She then cleaned the kitchen and walked to the studio to retrieve her sketchpad. She sat beside the bed and marveled at the raven-haired beauty that was fast asleep. The robe had fallen open when she lay back on the bed. The gold locket her father had given her glistened brightly on her chest. Milly's hand began to move as she penciled the outline of the bed and then the beautiful woman lying in it. She drew for hours until she was satisfied with the rendering, deciding that she would begin the painting later in the day.

She carefully crept into the bed beside Sasha and curled her body around her, snuggling into her warmth. She closed her eyes and allowed her body to drift into sweet dreams of herself and Sasha, holding hands as they walked through the streets of Paris.

†

The next few days passed quietly as Sasha regained her strength. Milly nursed her night and day and painted while she rested. On the fourth day after her rebirth, Milly brought the carriage around to the flat, and she and Sasha drove around the city as Sasha adjusted to her heightened senses. At first, Sasha had to shade her eyes from the bright sunlight, but they eventually became accustomed to the light. Sasha could hear every movement surrounding her and at times would cover her ears to lessen the pain.

"Focus and block the sounds with your mind, Sasha," Milly instructed. After several failed attempts, Sasha could begin to make the more prominent sounds fade to the background until the noise level was tolerable.

Hundreds of heartbeats and the rushing of blood through the crowd's veins assaulted Sasha's ears as Milly drove the carriage into the market district. The sound was thunderous and near maddening to Sasha and she begged Milly to leave the area.

Sasha looked exhausted by the ordeal so Milly turned the carriage and headed back to the flat. Sasha crept onto the bed and slept for several hours before her hunger woke her.

†

Each day they ventured farther and longer into the crowded streets of London and Sasha's strength and abilities improved with each passing day. Sasha could feel a burning sensation growing in her stomach that food did not quench and she told Milly of the hunger.

"It is time we hunt," Milly said. "Tonight we will go out together and you will experience your first feeding."

"Where will we go?" Sasha asked.

"At the edge of town is a tavern that serves many travelers and is in a remote location," she said. "There we will begin our hunt tonight, but for now you must sleep."

†

In the darkest hours of the morning, Milly woke Sasha with a kiss. "It is time, my love," she whispered.

Sasha climbed from the bed and dressed warmly, for the night was cool. She and Milly left the flat and walked through the fog-filled night until they reached the tavern Milly had spoken of earlier. They waited in the shadows and watched as the men began to leave the tavern for parts unknown.

Within an hour, an older man with a racking cough stumbled from the tavern and looked up and down the streets. "He is dying from within," Milly said quietly to Sasha. "If he heads out of town, we will follow him."

Sasha watched as the man turned away from town and began to stumble his way over broken cobbles, and when she looked at Milly, she nodded her head. They allowed the man a few minutes lead to make sure no other patrons would follow shortly behind him and then they stepped out of the shadows.

They walked quickly and Sasha could hear the beating of the man's weak heart as they approached. Her body was on fire as the bloodlust consumed her and her pace quickened. She and Milly caught the man and led him into a dense forested area off the road. The man was oblivious to what was about to occur to him and allowed them to lead him deeper into the woods.

Sasha looked at Milly when they stopped and saw that her eyes were aglow with excitement.

Milly would allow Sasha the kill and intervene only if necessary to prevent detection. She nodded to Sasha and Sasha knew it was time to make her first kill.

Sasha turned to face the old man and his blue eyes sparkled with what little life he had in him.

"Are you the angel of death, come to carry me away?" he asked.

"Yes," Sasha said, and she bent over the man and sank her fangs into his neck, tasting her first human blood. Her mind again swirled with waves of red and white lights as she drank from his body, quenching the burning need deep within her. She listened as his heart raced faster as it tried to increase the flow of oxygen to his body and then slowly faded until his life was no more. Sasha held the frail man in her arms and then licked the wound until the bruised, torn flesh healed. With Milly's aid, she placed the man under an ancient tree. The man wore a smile on his face that gave Sasha comfort, knowing that he was happy to be free of this life.

"You did well," Milly said. "How do you feel?"

"I feel so powerful," Sasha said as she joined her lover. "I feel he was ready to pass from this world, and in a bizarre way I feel that I did him a service."

"He was suffering great pain and would not have lived much longer," Milly said to ease Sasha's concern. "You allowed him to pass on in happiness and not in pain."

They walked back into the city in silence. They were passing a small garden when Sasha felt a strange tingling in her head. She looked at Milly who smiled and said, "There is another immortal among us." She touched Sasha's temple and said, "You will feel a tingling sensation right here when another is close by."

"I do not feel that when I am with you," Sasha said.

"That is because I made you, and you will always have a connection to me, my love," Milly said. "However close or far apart we are, we will always have the ability to project and read each other's thoughts."

Sasha grinned. Do you know how much I love you then? Sasha projected.

Enough to spend eternity with me, Milly answered with her mind and then took Sasha in her arms to share a deep kiss. They returned to the flat, undressed, and loved the remainder of the night away.

Chapter Ten

War Comes to England

The months flew by and Sasha became adjusted to her new abilities and needs. In late December as they prepared for the Christmas holiday, they were disturbed from their dinner meal by the blaring of sirens, which sounded as a German air raid occurred on English soil. Milly and Sasha hovered in a small closet in the studio for hours until the sirens vanished and the night became still again. The German bombs had not reached London; however, they heard their explosions from miles distant.

Sasha found it hard to believe that whole continents would be involved in a war. "I can't believe the whole world has gone crazy and this conflict continues," Sasha groaned.

"Some of these nations have been fighting for years and like a virus the infection has spread like wildfire," Milly said with a sad tone in her voice. "Mankind has proved through the centuries that it cannot exist without war."

As the raids continued, Sasha became infuriated by the reality that the safety of her world in London was being threatened. "This is entirely foolish," she said to Milly one night as they huddled together and listened to explosions in the distance.

Several more raids occurred over the next few months. London was spared repeatedly from the devastation, but it would only be a matter of time. Sasha read the papers fervently for news of the battles and her heart ached for the families of the thousands killed or wounded and the entire towns laid waste by the raging war. Her sensitive nature could not fathom so many innocent lives ruined by the cruelty of humankind. One particular article showed photographs of a small Russian village that had been bombed and the ground was littered with the bodies of women and children. She lay weeping in Milly's arms for hours that evening as her heart mourned their loss.

"Why do men have to be so ignorant?" Sasha asked.

"I wish I had the answer to that question, my love," Milly said as she soothed away her lover's tears.

†

They were dining at home one evening when a knock came at the door of the flat. Milly opened the door to find a young messenger standing there.

"I have a transatlantic cable for Miss Sasha Thibodaux," he said.

"Sasha, it is for you," Milly said as she walked back into the flat.

Sasha walked to the door and smiled at the young man who was holding the small envelope in his hand. "I am Sasha Thibodaux," she said.

"Good evening, miss, I have a cable for you," he repeated. "I must have your signature though, miss," he said with a slight stutter and handed her a receipt to sign.

Sasha smiled and took the board from the young man and placed her signature on the receipt as requested. He then handed her the envelope and, with a quick nod, the young man was gone. Sasha closed the door behind him and joined Milly on the couch. She opened the envelope and found that the message was from her father. Sasha read his message aloud to Milly.

My Dearest Daughter,
The news we receive about the battles in Europe grows
increasingly grave. I am writing to implore you and Milly
to come home when you can. Many nations have joined this
great struggle that they are now calling the Great War, and
I fear for your and Milly's safety if you choose to remain.
Please heed my warning and come home before it is too
late to safely travel.
Your Loving Father

Milly placed her hand on Sasha's. "He's right, you
know, armies are swarming like nests of angered hornets
and it will be devastating to the countries of Europe," she
warned. "You should answer your father and tell him that
you will sail for America as soon as possible."

"What about you?" Sasha said, confused by Milly's
statement. "You promised to go with me."

"I will join you as I promised, but first I have
obligations I must meet. I will return to you just as quickly
as I can."

"I will wait for you then," Sasha said. "I will not leave
without you."

"No, my love, you must go home. I will follow shortly
and we will begin a new life in America," Milly said.

"But I want to travel with you," Sasha insisted. "I will
be safe with you and when your business is complete, we
can travel together."

"Americans will be more the target now as Germany is
trying to entice them into this battle, and it will not be safe
for you to stay, my love, and I will not take no for an
answer."

Sasha knew there would be no arguing the point with Milly. Angered by Milly's stubbornness, Sasha would resign herself to Milly's point of view.

"We will inquire about a travel schedule tomorrow and then you can answer your father with the itinerary," Milly said. "I will also set my plans in motion and should only be a few weeks behind you at most."

"But—" Sasha started to say, and was cut off by Milly.

"Please, Sasha, just do this for me," Milly asked.

"Fine then," Sasha said and remained quiet the rest of the evening as she sulked.

Milly could not help but smile at Sasha as she pouted so diligently. "My love, you know I would not ask you to do this if I was not worried for your safety," Milly said.

"I know, Milly, but that doesn't mean I have to like it," Sasha said.

Milly pulled Sasha to her and kissed her deeply. Sasha was reluctant to leave her behind, but she would do as Milly asked. She held Sasha in her arms later that evening and whispered, "We will be together forever as promised, my love."

✝

The next day they made the travel arrangements for Sasha to return home. Ships outward bound from Liverpool were booked for the next few weeks as tourists and Americans were fleeing Europe, so they booked the next available berth. They also made Milly's arrangements to travel to Christiania in Norway for the same day. She would remain there for two weeks for her final showing and then after a brief stop in Ireland, would return to England to sail to America. Milly booked her trip to America at the same time so Sasha would know what her travel plans would be and lessen some of her anxiety. When they returned to the flat, they began sorting through their belongings. They determined which items they would ship to America and those they would sell, or give away to the needy.

Sasha could not believe the amount of personal belongings she had accumulated in such a short time. Even the smallest of trinkets held sentimental value for her and she ended up packing much more than she planned for shipment to the United States.

Milly would take the paintings she had stored in the studio and hope all or most of them would sell in Norway. Together, they would ship fifteen trunks on a commercial freighter that would depart London just before Sasha. If they were fortunate, the trunks would arrive in New Orleans shortly after Sasha, who would travel with the maximum two trunks allowed on the steamer.

That evening Sasha wrote her cable to Theo, deciding to travel downtown to send it the next morning. Later that night they hunted together for the last time in London, taking a pair of drunken sailors and dropping their bodies into the Thames.

†

The days passed quickly and then it was departure day for them. Sasha walked around the flat that morning, sad that their life here was ending. They had shared so much in the flat. She would always cherish it in her memory as their first home.

"I absolutely hate that we are being forced to leave our home," Sasha told Milly. "Life has been so perfect for us here."

"I know, my darling, but we have an opportunity for a new start in a country where we will be safe from harm," Milly said.

Sasha had no doubt that they would find a beautiful home in New Orleans and that hope kept her from flooding the room with tears. When the time came to depart for the station, Milly took Sasha in her arms and kissed her passionately. "I love you and will see you in New York in just a few weeks," Milly said.

"Those will be the longest weeks of my life," Sasha said as her eyes welled with tears.

"This will be the last time we will ever be apart," Milly said as she held her lover close.

They walked to the station through a light mist. They cherished the train ride to Liverpool and walked solemnly together to the harbor. Milly's ship left before Sasha's and Sasha clung to her until the final moment came for boarding. "Will you change your mind and come with me please?" Sasha pleaded for the last time.

"I cannot, my love, but I will be by your side soon," Milly said and with a soft kiss, she turned to board the ship.

Sasha felt her heart tearing from her chest as she watched her love on deck until the ship sailed out of sight. With tears flowing down her cheeks, she walked to the section of the port where her ship would depart and was given permission to board and led to her cabin. Sasha lay down on the bed and cried herself to sleep. When she awoke, the ship had sailed and she felt the familiar rocking of the ship as it sliced through the water. She reached out with her mind and felt Milly's presence. *I love you and miss you dearly,* she projected.

Milly smiled as she watched the gulls dive in front of fishing boats as her ship skirted the coast. *I love you too, and I'm wrapping my arms around you, holding you close,* she answered.

Sasha could feel the sensation of Milly's arms around her body and she let her body relax. She would sleep deep into the night and then get up to write in her diary until the sun rose the next morning. The early spring seas were turbulent and it was difficult to remain on deck, so Sasha returned to her cabin after the morning meal. Milly would be reaching her destination today and would begin preparation for her showing. Sasha would busy herself with writing and dreaming of their life in New Orleans.

✝

The days passed slowly and when Sasha went on deck and finally saw the outline of land ahead, she let out a deep sigh of relief. She stepped off the ship, glad to have her feet on solid ground. She would spend the night at the Alyson Boarding House with Joshua and Ella, who were now the owners of the establishment. They had arranged for her to stay in her old room for the evening, and the following morning they would take her to the train station, just as they had done many times while she lived in New York.

Ella was the first to see Sasha and her squeals of delight rang in Sasha's ears as the woman hugged her tight. "It is so good to see you again," she said. "You have grown into such a beautiful young woman."

Sasha hugged the woman tightly. "It is good to see you and Joshua again too. I have missed you so since I left the States."

Joshua hugged Sasha and said, "It's good that you have finally come home. It has become too dangerous in Europe these days."

"Oh Joshua, you can't imagine the devastation that is occurring over there," Sasha said as she stepped back. "It is all so senseless."

"I pray each day that we never have to experience another war on our cherished land," Joshua said as he led the two women to the waiting carriage. "There has been enough blood spilled on this soil to last for eternity."

Sasha was amazed at how the city had grown since she had first sailed to London. "This place has changed so much," she said as Joshua clicked his tongue at the horses to get them moving.

"Immigrants from Europe continue to flock to America and many have decided to stay in New York City, eager to make new lives for themselves," Joshua said as he guided the carriage along broad avenues that were now filled with carriages and the massive first rumblings of motorized vehicles.

When they arrived at the boarding house, Joshua carried her bags to her room. It had not changed since she lived there and a flood of memories besieged her as she sat at the desk she had used for her studies. Joshua quietly closed the door and left Sasha to her memories.

†

Sasha joined them in the kitchen half an hour later and sat with Joshua as Ella finished preparing their meal. They feasted on roast pork and vegetables, the same meal served the first night Sasha had stayed here in her youth. She smiled with the comfort of that memory and of meeting Amelia for the first time. Several years had passed since Sasha had thought of her, and she wondered what she would be like now.

"Tell us about life in London," Ella said to bring her back to reality.

"London is such an amazing place, Ella. You and Joshua would have loved it there before the war," she said. "The culture there is so different, it is almost impossible to describe."

"How much did you get to travel while you were there?" Joshua asked.

"I saw most of France, England, Ireland, and some parts of Norway," she answered. "Paris is such a romantic city and the food there is unforgettable. I think Europeans, as a rule, have a better appreciation of the arts, and their performance venues are like none I have ever seen here."

"Well, maybe now that you are back in the States, you can change that. You always were the best and I am sure you have only improved since the time you spent here," he said proudly.

"Thank you, Joshua," Sasha said. "I hope to be able to do some touring once we get settled in New Orleans."

"Once we...?" Ella asked.

"A most amazing woman named Milly Vansant will be joining me in New Orleans," Sasha said. "She is a fantastic painter and should be sailing here in just a few weeks."

Ella and Joshua could hear the excitement Sasha had in her voice when she talked about Milly, and they knew their young friend was deeply in love. "Both of you will have to make plans to visit then once you are settled," Ella said.

"I would like that, Ella," Sasha said. "You and Joshua mean so much to me, and I would love for Milly to meet you."

"We will look forward to it then," Joshua said and Ella nodded her head in agreement.

They sat and talked for hours until Sasha's travel-weariness overcame her and she found herself yawning.

"Why don't you head off to bed and we will see you for breakfast," Ella suggested.

Sasha crept into bed and was asleep almost as soon as her head hit the pillow. She dreamed of making love with Milly and when she awoke the next morning, she could taste Milly's sweet kisses on her lips. *I love you,* she sent across the ocean.

I will love you forever, Milly projected back.

†

Sasha packed her bag and after a hot breakfast, Joshua took her to the train station. Ella had tears in her eyes as Sasha hugged her goodbye. "Come back soon," she said as she walked them to the door.

"I will. I plan to return to New York to meet Milly when she arrives," Sasha said as she followed Joshua out the door.

At the station, Joshua walked her to the train and before hugging her goodbye said, "It is so good to see you happy again, Sasha. I look forward to seeing you soon and meeting this Milly of yours."

"Count on it," Sasha said, and with a final embrace she climbed aboard the train and watched as Joshua walked back to the carriage, and pulled away.

Sasha quickly found that New York City was not the only place that had grown wildly in her absence. The countryside had changed so vastly since her youth, but she remained entranced by the steadfast mountains and endless valleys. She was happy to see the expanding population did not yet inhabit them. How much of New Orleans would have changed, she wondered, as she found her sleeping cabin and retired for the night.

Chapter Eleven

Home

New Orleans had indeed changed. Sasha hardly recognized the train station. It had grown so enormous and there were trains everywhere. It took several minutes to find her father in the bustling crowd that had gathered to greet her fellow passengers. As handsome and charming as ever, Theo waved and rushed to greet his daughter.

"It is so good to see you, Sasha. I am happy you heeded my warning and came home." He looked confused when he looked around and could not find Milly. "Where is Milly?" he asked.

"She is not with me, Father, but she will be here in a few weeks," Sasha said.

Theo scowled at her response, silently fearful for his daughter's friend. "That won't be long then," he said cheerfully to hide his misgivings as he located a porter.

Theo arranged for the delivery of her trunks to their home and then he and Sasha began their walk. They strolled down past the harbor, which had also grown to giant proportions as transporting goods down the Big Muddy had exploded with international trade. They turned a corner and Sasha stopped dead in her tracks, staring at the building looming in front of her eyes.

"Our new office," Theo said.

"Father, it is beautiful," Sasha exclaimed as she walked faster to keep up with an excited Theo.

Theo held the door open for his daughter and watched as her face lit with excitement while she scanned the expanse of the new office. The wide-open floor plan allowed Theo a clear view of the entire office and he could monitor the shipping clerks he now employed. Next to Theo's large desk was an identical desk, with a nameplate, which bore the name Sasha Thibodaux.

"Welcome home," Theo said as he pulled a rolling chair covered in leather from under the desk.

"Of course I don't expect you to start work right away, but we are all set when you are ready," he said.

"So much has changed. It will probably take me months to learn about all the changes," Sasha said.

"Still all the basics you know so well, we just do them a little differently now. You will have these new machines mastered in days," Theo said confidently to his daughter. "But now, I must get you home as your mother is so anxious to see you. I will show you around on Monday."

Ten minutes later they were walking through the gate in the front yard and found Marie was eagerly waiting for them on the front porch, a pitcher of lemonade sitting beside her. She poured them glasses when she saw them enter through the gate and embraced her daughter. "Welcome home, Sasha, but where is Milly?" she asked.

Sasha was pleased that both her parents had inquired about Milly so quickly. "She had some final business to take care of, but she should be here in a few weeks," Sasha said.

"Wonderful," Marie said, truly relieved. "It will be so good to have you both in the house." "Thanks, Mother," Sasha said, adding, "Milly and I will be looking for a place of our own when she arrives."

"Really," Theo said as he set Sasha's bag on the porch. "The Milford place just down the street is for sale."

"That might be just the place for us," Sasha said with a bright smile.

"We will have to inquire about it then," Theo said as he sat next to his daughter.

It felt good to be at home, but she missed Milly dearly. She rocked on the porch, talked with her parents until dinnertime, and then after the meal excused herself for the evening.

She dressed in her nightclothes and lay down on the bed. She reached out with her mind and searched for Milly.

I love you, my darling she projected.

I love you too, Sasha, are you home yet? Milly asked.

Yes, just today, and we are all eager for your arrival, Sasha answered.

Just a few more days and I will leave for Ireland and then back to London, Milly said.

Not soon enough for me, Sasha said. Kiss me good night.

Sasha could feel Milly's soft lips pressing onto hers and could taste the sweetness of Milly as she closed her eyes and felt the kiss.

Goodnight, my love, Milly said.

Sasha ached to hold Milly in her arms and relieve the longing that was gnawing at the pit of her stomach. With great effort, Sasha willed her body to sleep.

✝

Sasha slept peacefully that night and when she awoke the next morning, she shared breakfast with her parents and then left the house to explore the city she loved. She walked to the cemetery first and visited her grandmother's grave. "It is good to be home again," she whispered as she bent down to kiss the headstone. "You would have loved Europe, Grandmother. I had such a wonderful time there and met the most amazing woman, who has stolen my heart. She makes me so happy and we will live together forever in love," Sasha said, the love shining in her eyes as she spoke softly of her beloved. "I will visit again soon and bring Milly by when she arrives."

Sasha walked down the streets one by one. She noted several new businesses and many grand new homes built in her absence. People were everywhere, on the streets, sitting on the balconies of homes and businesses and her head swam with all the new stimuli. Sasha sat on a nearby bench until her head cleared and then she continued her stroll. Several times during her walk, she felt the familiar tingling of another immortal and made a mental note to seek them out once Milly arrived.

Sasha walked home and took a route that would take her past the Milford House. She stopped on the sidewalk in front of it and was pleased with its appearance. The gardens were immaculate and the house would be large enough for the both of them. Smiling broadly, Sasha walked the remainder of the way home as she daydreamed of a new home for her and Milly.

✝

Sasha slept late the next morning and was content to spend the day visiting with her parents in the garden, enjoying the low humidity of a late spring day. There would be few of these days ahead with summer approaching and they felt privileged to have such mild weather.

"I can't believe how beautiful the weather is today, Father."

"We had better enjoy it while we can, the summer is predicted to be a brutal one," he said. "The humidity will be so thick when you step outside you will feel like you are walking into an oven."

"Thanks for such a pleasant preview," Marie teased as she refilled their tea glasses.

They sat in the garden until well after nightfall and then retired into the house for dinner. After assisting her mother with cleaning up the kitchen, Sasha walked back out into the garden and sat down, gazing up into the heavens. "I hope you are seeing this beautiful night sky filled with so many stars," Sasha said aloud as she thought of Milly.

†

Monday morning, Sasha was awake and, much to Theo's surprise, ready to go to work.

"Are you sure you wouldn't rather rest a few more days?" Theo asked.

"No, Father, if you do not mind, I would rather stay busy until Milly arrives, to help keep my mind occupied," Sasha said.

"Very well then," Theo said with a smile, and with a goodbye to Marie, they left for the office.

"Thank you, Father," Sasha said as they walked to the office.

"For what?" he asked.

"For allowing me to keep my mind busy," she said with a grin.

"I know patience was never one of your better qualities," Theo said with a chuckle as he placed his arm around her shoulders.

When they arrived at the office, Theo spent the first part of the morning showing Sasha around and demonstrating the use of the new machinery.

Sasha indeed was a fast learner and with minor instruction, she began sending cables and typing shipping orders as they arrived. She also worked to set up an inventory system to enable Theo to track stores in his warehouse. It felt good to be working with her father again, and he had to drag her away from the desk when the day was done.

"There will still be plenty to do tomorrow," Theo said with a chuckle.

As they began the short walk home, Theo smiled at his daughter. "I will be taking the train up to Baton Rouge on Wednesday to discuss a new contract if you would care to join me."

"That sounds like it would be fun," Sasha said.

"Good, we will go to the station in the morning and arrange our tickets then," Theo said as he placed his arm around her shoulders. "It is so good to have you home."

"It is good to be here too," Sasha said. "Europe was fantastic, but as you told me years ago, Nawlins will always be home."

Theo smiled at his daughter, and they enjoyed the early evening air as they walked home.

After dinner, Theo sat out on the front porch to read the evening paper. He would sometimes smoke a pipe as he read and Sasha remembered the smell from her childhood as she sat in the swing with her mother. She watched Theo's brow furrow as he read and made several grunting sounds.

"The world has gone mad," he said as he folded the paper and placed it on the table beside him. Shaking his head in disgust he said, "I don't understand why these nations must make war to prosper. It isn't as if Germany and other countries are running out of space or anything."

"I fear we will never understand the motivations of mankind, Father," Sasha said. "There have always been wars since there has been written record and I honestly don't see that changing anytime soon."

"Unfortunately I agree with you, Sasha," Theo said with sadness evident in his voice and then he fell silent.

The chirping of crickets and the lonely sound of a barge horn as it sailed down the Big Muddy sounded loud in the silence. "I hope this madness will be limited to Europe and it will have a minimum of effect on the States," Theo eventually said as he puffed on his pipe.

Marie and Sasha nodded in agreement and continued to swing and enjoy the cool night.

†

The next morning, Theo and Sasha bought their tickets for the train ride to Baton Rouge for the following day, and Sasha also bought a ticket to New York for the coming Sunday. She would travel to New York to meet Milly and bring her home.

The day passed quickly as Sasha hoped and when she retired that evening, she tried to reach out to Milly. She could feel her presence, but not clearly enough to read or project into her thoughts. Sasha drifted off to sleep, worried for her love and wondering what she might be experiencing.

The next morning, Sasha again attempted to contact Milly and reached only a pool of blackness. She dressed and joined her parents downstairs with a growing sense of dread.

†

The trip to Baton Rouge was just what Sasha needed to take her mind off missing Milly. The day was bright and cool and when Theo led her into the office of the new client, Sasha felt the tingling of a fellow immortal. When they entered the office of Miss Owens, Sasha made eye

101

contact with the woman, and knew immediately whom the immortal was she sensed. "Louisa Owens," the woman said as she reached her hand out to shake his.

"Theo Thibodaux and my daughter and partner, Sasha Thibodaux," Theo said in return.

Louisa fixed her nearly black eyes on Sasha and smiled warmly as she took her hand. *Welcome sister,* she projected to Sasha. "So pleased to meet you both," she said aloud and offered them a seat.

Thank you for your welcome, Sasha returned silently. She listened to Theo's presentation and his conversation with the woman, while closely observing Louisa. Quite handsome and a powerful business mind, she thought as she listened to Louisa and Theo discussing prices and quantities of cane and cotton that would be shipped. After an hour of conversation, it appeared Louisa and Theo had come to an agreement, and he pulled out a contract that both of them signed.

"It is a pleasure doing business with the Thibodaux family," Louisa said. "Will you allow me to treat you to lunch while you are in our fair city?"

"That would be lovely, but I must insist on paying," Theo said.

Louisa, Theo, and Sasha shared a fantastic meal of red beans and rice with spicy Cajun sausage, fresh French bread, and drank sweet tea until midafternoon. The conversation remained light as they ate. Theo had taught Sasha that it was improper to discuss business over such a fine meal. "I hope the next time you travel to Nawlins you will stop in for a visit," Theo said as they said their farewells.

"You can count on that," Louisa said with a chuckle as she shook Theo's hand.

Be well until we meet again, my sister, she projected to Sasha.

I will be looking forward to the day, Sasha returned in response.

Theo and Sasha walked to the train station and awaited their return trip to Nawlins. "You are an incredibly shrewd businessman, Father," Sasha said as they sat together.

"Miss Owens is quite a match for me." He chuckled. "She almost had me below my bottom line price there for a while," Theo said as he safely tucked the new contract inside his jacket pocket.

"But she didn't, Father," Sasha said as she chuckled.

They returned to New Orleans and got home just as Marie was setting the table for dinner.

"Well, you two have excellent timing," she said as she welcomed her family home.

That evening, Sasha went to bed with her head swimming with her first encounter with another immortal besides Milly. She had tried several times during the day to reach Milly, but there seemed to be a strange interference. As she lay still in bed, she relaxed and felt the familiar buzzing sensation of Milly entering her mind. *Ah, there you are, dear,* Milly said.

Oh, Milly, you had me so worried, Sasha said.

I don't know what is happening, but there is some sort of astral interference going on. I have been trying to reach you for two days, Milly replied.

Likewise, but it is good to hear from you finally. Are you all right? Sasha asked.

Yes, I am fine and will be sailing to Ireland tomorrow, Milly said.

Good, I cannot wait until you arrive safely. Milly, you had me so worried.

Relax, my love, I will be there within the week, Milly said to assure Sasha that everything was fine. She could feel her lover's anxiety and her soft words did little to put Sasha at ease.

I just have a horrible feeling that something bad is about to happen, Sasha said.

Do not dwell on it, my love, I will be there soon, Milly said, then their contact was broken.

Sasha tried her best to relax, but despite her efforts, her dreams were filled with death and doom. She awoke covered in perspiration, fearful of more dreams, decided to stay up the rest of the night. Sasha dressed and spent the remainder of the night sitting on the front porch, listening to the nighttime chorus until the sun began to rise above the horizon.

†

Theo could sense the anxiety coming from his daughter the next morning and saw that she was having great difficulty concentrating on her tasks. "Are you feeling all right, Sasha?" he asked later during the day.

"No, Father, I sense that something terrible is about to occur, but I don't know exactly what it will be," she said.

"Well, it is already late in the afternoon, so why don't you take the rest of the day and go for a stroll to see if you can sort out your thoughts," he suggested.

Sasha thanked her father for the suggestion, and, after saying her goodbyes to the staff, she left the office and walked toward the levee. She walked the levee until the sun started to set and then turned toward the Garden District and walked through the streets filled with beautiful homes and fragrant gardens. She concentrated on her thoughts, but could not make any sense of what was coming to bear. It was well past dinnertime when Sasha, frustrated, finally turned for home.

When she stepped through the front gate and found her parents waiting for her on the porch, Sasha knew from the look on her father's face that something was drastically wrong.

As she stepped up to the porch, Sasha saw the newspaper still in Theo's hand and read the headline: *Lusitania Sunk by German Torpedo.*

"Oh no, please say it can't be true! That is Milly's ship, she was returning to London on it," she said as she took the paper from Theo and read. *A German submarine torpedo sank the British passenger liner, the Lusitania, as it sailed off the southwest coast of Ireland.* Sasha groaned as she read. *Eleven hundred ninety-eight passengers and crew confirmed as dead.*

Sasha read those last words and gasped. She fainted and Theo was barely able to catch her before she struck the ground.

Chapter Twelve

The Mourning Begins

Theo carried Sasha to her bed and watched over her for hours while she showed no signs of waking. His heart ached for his daughter's loss, and he felt helpless as he sat next to her bed.

Marie had brought the paper up to Sasha's room and Theo reread the article, trying to will the devastating news away. The Germans declared they had sent warnings regarding using passenger ships for transporting Allied soldiers, and they sank the *Lusitania* because they thought the crew was British sailors. An unfortunate and fatal error for the nearly twelve hundred passengers and their loved ones, but Germany was not going to issue an apology or admit an error.

"Damn, those arrogant Germans," Theo said loudly.

Theo continued reading the article, and the reporter stated that inside sources in Washington had revealed that the President and his advisers were meeting to determine whether the United States would now join in the great World War. Over one hundred of the Lusitania's passengers had been Americans, and it was highly improbable that the President would allow the outright murder of his nation's citizens to go unpunished. Theo's heart continued to sink as he read the words, his worst fears coming to life.

Sasha groaned, bringing his attention back to his daughter and the heartbreak she was suffering. Marie came into the room near daybreak and handed Theo a small hypodermic. Their family physician had dropped by on Theo's request and after a quick examination of Sasha, determined she was suffering from severe shock. The physician had left a dose of a sedative for Sasha if she awoke in a fit of hysterics or if she were unable to rest peacefully. Theo prayed he would not have to administer the medicine to his daughter, but was comforted to have it if needed. Marie, worried for both her husband and her daughter, held vigil with Theo throughout the remainder of the morning, refilling their coffee mugs several times during the ordeal.

Together they watched as Sasha thrashed in the bed. Her dreams filled with the nightmare of losing Milly in that horrible fashion. Her body covered with perspiration, and she occasionally called out Milly's name in agony. Theo could take no more of his daughter's pain and, with Marie's assistance, administered the injection as the physician had instructed.

Within ten minutes, Sasha's body relaxed and she fell into a deep sleep, undisturbed by her horrific dreams. Theo sent Marie off to bed and allowed his exhausted eyes to close as he sat next to his daughter.

Six hours later, Theo woke to the sound of Sasha's sobs as she read the newspaper he had left beside her bed. Theo went to his daughter and held her in his arms as her body shook with the convulsions of her emotional trauma. "I am so sorry," Theo repeated as he and Sasha rocked on the bed.

"Why, Father?" Sasha asked, knowing that her father could not answer the question.

"I do not know, Sasha," Theo answered with tears running down his cheeks.

"Why now? Why my Milly, Father?" Sasha groaned as Theo held her in his arms.

They remained like that for another hour, a father holding his daughter as they cried together, suffering for their loss. Marie had also woken and gone to the kitchen to prepare sandwiches and soup in the hope Sasha would try to eat something.

With encouragement from her parents, Sasha ate half a sandwich and sipped on the soup as they sat on her bed, but Sasha's stomach revolted and she ran to the bathroom to purge the food from her stomach. Covered in perspiration again and feeling horribly weak, Sasha allowed Theo to assist her back to her bed.

Sasha slipped quickly back to sleep, clutching a pillow tightly to her body for comfort. Marie, worried about Theo, sent him off to bed with a promise that she would wake him if Sasha woke again. The dark circles under his eyes gave away his exhausted state and within minutes of lying down, he was softly snoring. Marie kissed his forehead and returned to Sasha's room to watch over her only child.

Marie leaned down and brushed the dark hairs away from Sasha's face, then sat next to the bed. Watching Sasha sleep, Marie felt as if it were mere days since Sasha was a child playing in the gardens and learning how to play the piano. It was difficult for her to adjust to her daughter being a grown woman and now suffering her greatest heartache. Marie had hoped that her daughter would find a nice young man and provide her with several grandchildren, but as time passed, she realized this dream would not come true. She had been happy for Sasha when she fell in love with Milly, but now worried how her daughter would survive such heartbreak.

✝

When Sasha awoke again, she managed to keep a small cup of soup in her system, but sat staring off into space for hours at a time.

Theo was worried that the strain of losing Milly had been too great for his daughter and that her mind had shut down to ease the pain. He knew he must get her up and moving about to prevent her from slipping further away from reality. He managed to get Sasha out to the front porch to sit on the swing in the sunshine for a few hours, which appeared to lighten her mood though she refused to speak.

Sasha had tumbled into a world of emotional darkness and her body ached with every movement. She was aware of Theo and his efforts to stimulate her senses, trying to bring her out of the fugue state she was lost in, but she could not break through the barrier.

Later that day Marie fed her spoonfuls soup that she instinctively swallowed. Theo was distraught, unable to break through to his daughter and as his frustration mounted, he thought of an idea.

"Marie, will you play for us?" Theo asked, hoping the music she so loved would lead Sasha back.

"Yes, dear, I will," Marie answered, and they walked into the parlor.

Theo and Sasha sat on the sofa as Marie sat on the bench in front of the piano. "Theo, bring her here," Marie said and Theo led Sasha over to sit beside her mother.

Sasha remained mute and sat holding her hands in her lap as Marie began to play. Theo watched Sasha closely, and as Marie played Sasha began to move with the rhythm of the music. He smiled with delight as the light in Sasha's eyes slowly returned and her fingers reached out to touch the solid keys. Marie continued to play and after several more minutes, Sasha's fingers began to move along the keys as she began to play. Marie continued to play until

Sasha's fingers were moving instinctively across the keys as she played the piece her mother had started. When she reached the end of the piece, Sasha looked over at Theo, then her mother, and smiled.

Sasha had returned.

Chapter Thirteen

Tragedy Escaped

Sasha remained relatively quiet for the next two days as she mourned Milly's loss. Theo did his best to engage his daughter in conversation, but Sasha refused to talk to him about her feelings. She walked the levee every day and tried her best to gather her thoughts. It was on the second day as Sasha was walking down the levee that she felt a strange sensation in her head. She dropped to her knees and willed her mind to relax, fearing her distraught mind was playing a cruel trick on her.

Sasha, dear, are you there? Milly projected.

Sasha nearly fainted with delight. *Milly, my love, is it really you?*

Yes, it is, my love. I have been trying to reach you for days to let you know I am still alive.

You are alive! Oh, my God, Milly, we thought you were dead, Sasha said.

I would have been if I had not heeded your warning. I chose not to board the Lusitania, and took passage on another ship instead, Milly said.

Thank God, where are you? Sasha asked.

I am still in Christiana. I will depart straight for America once they allow us to travel again. Everything is still quite chaotic here, as you might expect, and they are arranging for naval escorts for ships traveling through the war zone, which will take a few more days. I have tried so desperately to contact you, but there is so much emotional turmoil going on blocking our contact. When I could reach you, I found that you were lost in a deep blackness, Milly said. *Are you well, my love?*

I am now, Sasha said. *I was quite disturbed by the news, as you might imagine. Father had to sedate me, then for a while I was just floating somewhere out in the blackness, unaware of anything going on. I am so relieved you are well, Milly, and cannot wait for you to get here, I miss you so.*

I miss you too, love, and I will let you know just as soon as I can travel, Milly promised and then the connection was gone. Sasha tried for several minutes to reconnect with Milly but her efforts were in vain. It mattered not, for Milly was alive and safe! Sasha stood and rushed to tell her parents of the news.

†

Marie opened the door and saw the messenger standing there. "I have a cable for Miss Sasha Thibodaux," the young man said.

"She is not here at the moment, but I will sign for it," Marie said, taking the receipt and signing it before taking the cable from him. The messenger thanked her and disappeared from the door as Marie stood looking at the small envelope. What news could this hold, she wondered. She carefully opened the envelope to find a brief note from Milly saying that she was alive and well and still in Christiania, having chosen not to board the *Lusitania*. Tears were flowing down her cheeks as Marie walked as fast as she could to Theo's office to find Sasha.

Theo saw his wife crying when she walked into the office and rushed to her side. "What is it?" he asked.

Marie was unable to speak so she handed the cable to Theo. Theo read the message, then picked up Marie and twirled his wife in the air with a loud whoop. "We must find Sasha and give her the news," he said as he led Marie to the door.

Theo and Marie started walking down the levee just as Sasha had done hours before. They walked for twenty minutes before they saw Sasha rushing toward them, wearing a huge smile.

"She's alive!" they could hear Sasha shout.

How was it possible that she knew the news when we have just received the cable, Theo wondered, but it did not matter enough for him to question.

"She's alive," Sasha repeated as she hugged her parents.

"We know," Theo said. "You just received this cable," he said as he handed the small slip of paper to her.

Sasha took the cable, read it, and clutched it to her chest. Happy tears flooded down her cheeks as they celebrated the fabulous news. Sasha read the cable repeatedly and her heart soared.

They walked downtown and had dinner out on the town to celebrate the good news. Theo was delighted to see his daughter smiling and laughing again during the meal and he knew all was right in her world.

Later that evening as Sasha lay in her bed, she again found the connection with Milly. They spoke for hours, each greatly relieved that the other was well and in good spirits. When Sasha finally slept that night, she clutched a pillow to her chest and dreamt of making love to Milly.

†

Two more days passed before Sasha received the next cable. Milly would depart Christiana the next morning and would arrive in New York the following Tuesday. Sasha planned to leave for New York on Saturday, which would allow her to arrive in plenty of time to meet Milly. Her excitement buzzed throughout the office for the rest of the week as she worked with Theo to keep her mind occupied. She was so excited she could barely sleep at night and decided she would feed before leaving for New York.

She awoke in the early hours of Saturday morning and crept quietly from the house. She walked down to the French Quarter and began her hunt. There would be plenty of partygoers leaving for home about this time and Sasha knew she would not be disappointed. She had also learned that she could feed without killing her prey, taking only what she would need to sustain herself. It left her victim weak and ill for a few days, but the encounter need not be fatal for them. Sasha would have to feed more frequently, but she preferred to hunt in this manner.

Sasha watched from the shadows as two women walked out of one of the taverns, and after speaking for several minutes, parted ways. She stepped out of the shadows behind the woman who had walked past her on her journey home and followed her until she slipped inside a small apartment. Sasha scanned the inside and found the woman lived alone and then boldly walked to the door and knocked. The woman opened the door to Sasha, transfixed by Sasha's eyes. Sasha closed the door behind her, led the woman into the small bedroom, and sat her on the bed. The woman smiled sweetly up at Sasha, who leaned down to kiss her soft lips. "I need something from you," she whispered to the woman, who sighed gently.

"Take what you need then," the woman answered and turned her head away from Sasha.

"Thank you," Sasha whispered and sank her fangs into the soft tissue of the woman's neck.

The woman moaned in pleasure as Sasha drank from her body. It was obvious to Sasha that this woman had volunteered as a feeder before, as she took such pleasure from Sasha's attentions. When Sasha had taken what she needed, she healed the wound and kissed the woman's lips again. "Sleep now, love," she said as she placed the woman back on the bed and covered her body with the soft linens. Sasha watched the woman as she slept sweetly and then left the apartment and headed for home.

Sasha could feel the faint tingling of another immortal as she slipped through the shadows and she knew she was not alone on the hunt tonight. Reaching home, she quietly slipped between her sheets and slept deep into the morning.

†

She joined Theo in the office for a few hours of work in the afternoon and then spent the remainder of the evening preparing for her trip to New York. She was awake before dawn, and after breakfast walked with her father down to the train station.

The train ride to New York passed quickly and her excitement continued to grow. Joshua met her at the station and she spent the first night explaining to them what had happened with Milly. They were both relieved that she had made it safely and looked forward to meeting Sasha's love.

On Monday, Sasha toured New York, amazed at how the city had changed in such a short time. She strolled through shops and galleries while searching for a special gift for Milly. She decided on a London-blue topaz ring that would match Milly's eyes and waited while the jeweler sized the ring and wrapped it in a small wooden box. Sasha returned to the boarding house and spent a quiet evening with Joshua and Ella before retiring to her room for a sleepless night.

†

Shortly before sunrise, Sasha climbed from the bed and walked down to the harbor. She sat on the seawall and watched a beautiful sunrise as it spread across the horizon, casting rays of yellow and orange across the deep blue water.

Very soon now, my love, Sasha sent across the water.

Yes, I should be able to see land in another hour.

I cannot wait to have you back in my arms again.

I promise I will never leave your arms again. Now our eternity shall begin, Milly said.

I love you, and will see you soon, Sasha said.

I love you too.

Sasha stared out across the open waters, silently willing Milly's ship to appear until her head began to hurt. She strolled down the pier and watched as fishermen unloaded their morning's catch of shrimp, fish, and lobster. Sasha bought four large lobsters and several pounds of shrimp and paid to have them delivered to Ella. They would share a quiet meal tonight, and Sasha felt the fresh seafood would be an excellent treat.

Sasha walked around the harbor for another hour then noticed that people had begun to gather to greet the arriving passengers, so she returned to her spot on the seawall to finish her wait.

Joshua arrived a while later with the carriage and joined Sasha on the seawall. "Ella said to thank you for the seafood, and that she would prepare you a feast to be remembered," he said as he sat beside her.

"I thought that would make a nice treat for us all," Sasha said to the smiling man.

"A fantastic treat, it's been some time since we have had fresh lobster. Ella is already making preparations for dinner," Joshua said with a chuckle.

When Sasha turned her attention back to the water, she could see the faint outline of a ship far off in the distance. "Look," she said to Joshua.

"I see it," Joshua said. "That has to be our ship."

The ship continued to grow on the horizon as they watched and when it was a few hundred yards from the harbor inlet, Joshua stood and offered his hand to Sasha. "Ready to go get your woman?" he asked.

"Yes, Joshua, I am," Sasha answered with a smile as she took his offered hand and allowed Joshua to help her stand. They walked to the end of the long pier where the ship would dock to resume their wait. Sasha could see Milly as she stood at the front of the large ship, waving excitedly to her love. "There she is, Joshua," Sasha said as she pointed Milly out to her friend.

"What a beauty she is, Sasha," he said.

"Yes, indeed Joshua, she is quite beautiful," Sasha agreed.

After what seemed like an eternity, the ship finally pulled up to the pier and men began to lash her to the moorings. The gangplank lowered and Milly rushed to be the first to disembark from the ship. She ran straight into Sasha's arms and embraced her tightly.

"I love you so, Sasha Thibodaux," she declared.

"I love you, Milly Vansant," Sasha softly whispered back to her lover.

When they ended their embrace, Sasha said, "Milly, this is Joshua."

"I feel as if I know you already," Milly said. "I have heard so much about you and Ella from Sasha."

"Likewise. Since Sasha has returned from Europe all she can talk about is you," Joshua teased. "Here, let me take that bag for you."

Joshua helped them into the carriage and arranged for the delivery of Milly's trunks to their house before climbing into the driver's seat. "A quick tour for you ladies?" he asked.

Both Milly and Sasha nodded their heads yes, and Joshua pulled the carriage onto the street. He drove them around the city for nearly two hours as Sasha excitedly pointed out landmarks to Milly.

✝

Ella met them at the door when she heard the carriage return and hugged Milly tightly. "It is so nice to finally meet you, Milly. I am glad you have arrived safely," Ella said as she led them into the foyer.

"Sasha will show you to your room and you ladies can catch up with one another while Joshua and I finish dinner," Ella said to the lovers.

"Are you sure you don't need our help?" Milly asked.

"No, dear. Joshua and I have cooked together for years and anyone else in my kitchen just gets in the way," Ella said with a laugh.

Sasha took Milly by the hand and led her into the bedroom. When she closed the door behind them, she took Milly in her arms and kissed her deeply as their bodies pressed against the door.

"Oh Milly, I feared I would never again taste your sweet lips," Sasha said with tears in her eyes.

Milly pulled her deeper into her embrace and searched her lover's eyes. "You will never have to fear that again," Milly said as she lowered her head and kissed Sasha.

Sasha pulled a small box from her pocket. "I bought you this to welcome you home."

Milly took the box and opened it to find the topaz ring Sasha had bought for her. She had tears flowing down her cheeks as she took the ring and handed it to Sasha. Sasha took the ring, slipped it onto Milly's left ring finger and smiled at the perfect fit. "I love you, Milly Vansant," Sasha said.

"I love you too, Sasha," Milly said as she embraced Sasha. "I will never be separated from you again, I promise."

Chapter Fourteen

A Longing Embrace

Dinner was excellent, just as Sasha knew it would be. They finished the lobsters and most of the shrimp during the meal. Milly had surprised them with a bottle of French wine that complemented the meal perfectly and they finished that as they talked around the table.

Milly and Sasha helped Ella clear the kitchen then they drank coffee with the couple before excusing themselves for the evening. Inside their room, Sasha slowly undressed Milly, taking special care to unfasten each button as her heart raced wildly. The silky smooth skin beneath her clothes begged for her lips and Sasha took her time in covering Milly with tender kisses as she undressed her lover. By the time Milly stepped out of her stockings, her body was quivering with anticipation. She sat on the edge of the bed and watched as Sasha removed her clothing and walked toward the bed.

"I have missed you so," Sasha said when she reached the bed.

"I know, but I am home now, my love," Milly said.

Sasha stood between Milly's knees and encircled her body with strong arms. Milly leaned forward and placed light kisses over Sasha's stomach and up to her breasts as her hands caressed down the back of her legs. Sasha buried her hands in the softness of Milly's hair as she watched her lover take a nipple in her mouth and begin to suckle. Her body burned with arousal as Milly's hand moved between them and stroked her wetness and then Milly's fingers gently entered her. Sasha moaned loudly as Milly moved deep inside her and rocked her hips in rhythm with Milly's thrusts.

Milly's teeth grazed Sasha's nipples and she began biting them as Sasha's inner muscles began to convulse around her probing fingers. Sasha cried out softly as her body released and she collapsed onto the bed with Milly. Milly pulled her on top of her body and held her lover as her body spasms continued.

Sasha's mouth found Milly's and her tongue parted her lips for a deep kiss as she ground her wetness into Milly. Milly's hands pulled Sasha's hips faster and faster against her body as they joined in sexual bliss. Sasha kissed her way down Milly's body until she reached the throbbing bud, swollen with need, and took it deep into her mouth, sucking it hard against the roof of her mouth. Milly's body writhed underneath her as Sasha parted her lower lips with trembling fingers that disappeared into the welcoming wetness. Milly's hands clenched the wrought-iron bedposts as her body bucked wildly, forcing Sasha's fingers deep inside her. Sasha's fangs were unsheathed as she pierced the blood-engorged bud and drank from her lover's body. "Oh yes, Sasha," Milly groaned as she buried her fingers in Sasha's hair, holding her close as Sasha feasted on her lover.

The combined taste of her lover's blood mixed with her excitement drove Sasha mad with pleasure as her body exploded in unison with Milly's. After Sasha recovered a bit, she softly licked the small wound and then climbed into Milly's arms. She laid her head upon Milly's chest and listened as their hearts beat as one. Milly looked into Sasha's lavender eyes as she reached down between Sasha's legs, and entered her again and thrust her wetness against Sasha's thigh. Sasha smiled and pressed her hand between her thighs and plunged into Milly as her hips undulated against her. They locked eyes as they gave one another pleasure again and then collapsed on the bed in a blissful embrace.

They held one another for hours, no words needed to express the love and devotion they shared. They slept until the sun rose and then headed to the bathroom to share a long soaking bath.

†

After breakfast, Joshua offered them the use of the carriage, but they refused, preferring to walk together instead as they resumed their tour of the city. For two days, they walked the streets of New York and spent their nights, after visiting with Joshua and Ella, loving one another late into the night.

Joshua had tears in his eyes when he dropped them at the train station. "I hope you two will come back and visit us soon," he said as he handed the women their bags.

"We will definitely be back," Milly said as she hugged Joshua.

"Thank you again for everything, Joshua," Sasha said as she embraced her good friend.

"It is always a pleasure."

Sasha and Milly boarded the train and turned to wave goodbye to Joshua. He returned their parting gesture and drove away from the station. They located their cabin and settled in for the trip. Sasha sat close to Milly and pointed out different locations throughout their trip. After dinner, they returned to their cabin and watched the landscape pass, wrapped in each other's arms. Later that night, their bodies joined the rocking of the train as they made love for hours before resigning themselves to sleep.

During the stop in Atlanta the next morning, Sasha and Milly departed the train to walk. It was a beautiful late spring day, the sky full of fluffy clouds moving briskly in the air as a cool breeze surrounded the lovers. They returned to the train just as the conductor was calling for all passengers to board and slipped quietly back into their cabin.

Sasha lay on her side next to Milly as the train pulled away from the station with a lurch and slowly began to pick up speed. The hand that had rested on Milly's hip slipped down between her legs and rocked with the motion of the train as it sped down the tracks. Sasha could feel the warmth growing under her hand as her lips found Milly's neck and she began to stroke her lover. "That feels so good, Sasha," Milly purred softly.

"I can make it feel so much better," Sasha whispered as her hand moved down to grasp the hem of Milly's dress and slowly slid it up her thighs to her waist.

Milly grasped the dress and held it above her waist as Sasha's fingers slowly traced the outline of her lips, which swelled with arousal and pressed tightly against the fabric of her panties. Milly's body thrummed with desire as Sasha slowly teased her lover, the nails of her fingers brushing lightly above the sensitive skin. "Feeling better yet?" she breathed.

"Oh yes, please do not stop, Sasha," Milly begged.

Sasha's fingers crept underneath the waistband of her panties and slowly worked them down Milly's hips as she raised them off the bed. Milly squirmed her way out of the panties, which landed across the cabin as Sasha's fingers brushed lightly across her exposed skin. She dragged the tips of her fingernails from hipbone to hipbone and then down to the crest of her mound. Milly's moans grew with each stroke of Sasha's hand.

Sasha allowed her fingertips to play in the soft, damp hairs as she moved closer to Milly's center much slower than Milly desired. "Please touch me," Milly said her voice slightly more than a whisper as her body trembled.

Sasha's fingers gently parted the swollen lips, caressing them with faint touches of her soft fingers. Milly's hips began to roll on the bed as she ached to have Sasha buried deep inside her needy body. Sasha draped her right leg over Milly's thighs, holding her hips on the bed. "We have hours yet before we arrive in New Orleans, my love, so there is no hurry," Sasha teased.

Milly relaxed her body and permitted Sasha's fingers to explore her body. Her body tormented by Sasha's touch, to the point she had to bite her lip to prevent herself from screaming and letting her body respond with an ear-shattering orgasm. Still, Sasha's fingers moved slowly and very deliberately into her body, raising her arousal to new heights. Sasha inserted one finger into the welcoming wetness and then a second as she caressed the inner walls of Milly's body. "More please," Milly groaned as Sasha slowly inserted a third finger, filling Milly completely, stretching her walls as she began moving in and out of her lover. Sasha's thumb rested comfortably on top of Milly's swollen bud and stroked across its tip with every movement of her hand.

It took great restraint to not rush Milly into a climax but Sasha patiently maintained a slow pace as she stroked deeply inside her lover. Sasha watched as Milly's hands covered her breasts and rubbed them roughly through her dress. Milly's eyes were an ocean-deep blue as they searched Sasha's, begging for release. A drop of blood formed on Milly's lip and Sasha leaned down to lick it away, then her tongue parted her lips and they kissed as

Sasha's fingers moved faster inside. Milly's moans vibrated in Sasha's mouth as they kissed deeper, and her pulsing inner muscles caressed Sasha's fingers as Milly's body erupted from within. She would have surely screamed out with pleasure had Sasha's tongue not been swirling deeply in her mouth.

Sasha broke the kiss and allowed Milly a chance to breathe. "Yes, my love," she said as her fingers remained inside Milly's body. She laid her head on Milly's chest and drifted into sleep, her fingers still inside her sated lover.

†

They awoke after sunset and went to the dining car for the evening meal. They would arrive in New Orleans in two hours, and Sasha was eager to show Milly her home.

"Milly, my love, Father has told me of a home for sale just down the street from them that I think is very beautiful. I would like for us to take a look at it," Sasha said. She told Milly what she knew about the Milford house and they agreed that they would make an appointment to see the house, and if it were as grand as Sasha described, they would make an offer to buy the home.

Milly could tell from Sasha's excitement that she wanted this to be their new home, and she would do anything to keep her lover happy.

The train rumbled across the great lake and Sasha knew she was nearly home. They would arrive later than she hoped, but there would be many days ahead for Sasha to show Milly around the city she loved. The lights of New Orleans began to flash by the cabin window as the train began to slow as it approached the station. Sasha and Milly packed their travel bags and waited patiently for the train to come to rest. Before they left the cabin, Sasha took Milly in her arms for a slow kiss. "There will be more of these later," she said as she took Milly's hand and led her through the train.

†

Theo was waiting for them as they stepped from the train, and he rushed to them and hugged them. "It is so good to have you both at home," he said, planting an excited kiss on each of their cheeks.

"It is great to finally be here," Milly said as she returned Theo's kiss.

"And not a moment too soon," Theo said. "The President announced today that the United States would be joining the war."

"Oh Father, I know that has been one of your fears from the beginning," Sasha said as she hugged him tight.

"It is all such nonsense," he said, shaking his head. "But, tonight I have my girls safely at home and that is all that matters."

They walked the short distance to their home and found Marie waiting for them on the porch. She hugged them close and welcomed Milly to their home. "We are so pleased to have you join us, Milly," she said.

"I appreciate you and Theo taking me into your home," Milly said.

"Nonsense," Theo chided with a smile. "You are a part of this family."

"Are you hungry?" Marie asked as she and Theo moved to sit in the rocking chairs that lined the porch. Milly and Sasha sat in the swing.

"I'm not, Mother," Sasha said. "We had dinner on the train." She looked at Milly, who shook her head as well.

"Your trunks were delivered this week and I had them placed in the warehouse," Theo said. "Are you still interested in the Milford house?"

"It sounds like such a lovely place," Milly said. "Sasha promised to take me by there tomorrow and then we will probably ask to tour the house."

"Well, I hope you don't mind, but I have already talked to the owner and have a key, if the two of you wanted to take a look around," Theo said with a grin. "Not that I am rushing you out of the house, but I know you will be more comfortable once you have your own place." Theo flushed with embarrassment.

Sasha grinned at her father, who was as excited about the house as she was. "Oh Father, you are always so considerate," Sasha said and kissed his cheek again. "Would you and Mother join us tomorrow then and give us your opinion?"

"We would love to, Sasha," Marie said, and Theo agreed.

"Well then, after breakfast, we will take a stroll," Theo said.

"Oh, and I was also talking with a friend who teaches at Tulane, and he says there are openings in the Art Department, if you are interested in continuing your teaching career, Milly," he said.

"I will look into that next week, Theo," Milly said.

Theo was overjoyed they had made it safely to New Orleans and would do anything in his power to help them settle in and feel comfortable. He hoped Sasha and Milly would never again leave if they had a home and careers in New Orleans.

Sasha knew exactly what her father was thinking and said, "Thank you for all that you have done."

"It has been my pleasure," Theo said.

Marie said, "It is getting late, Theo, so why don't you carry the girls' bags up to their room, and we will see them in the morning for breakfast."

"Yes, my love," Theo said and kissed all of them on the cheek as he stood and disappeared inside the house.

"Lock up when you come inside," Marie said. She stopped at the door and said, "It really is nice to have you both at home."

Sasha smiled at her mother and said, "Thank you, Mother; it is good to be home."

"Goodnight Marie," Milly said and with another smile, Marie left the porch.

Sasha sat back in the swing and placed her arm around Milly's shoulder. The night was very comfortable and they gazed upward to a sky lit by a full moon and a blanket of brilliant stars.

"It is so beautiful here," Milly said as she snuggled next to Sasha.

"Just wait, there is so much more for you to see," Sasha said.

"All I need is sitting right here beside me," Milly said sweetly.

Sasha looked into the deep blue eyes that locked with hers. "I know that feeling," she said, and hugged Milly close.

Chapter Fifteen

A New Beginning

Sasha and Milly dressed and joined Sasha's parents downstairs for breakfast. Theo was so excited he could barely contain himself as he downed his breakfast and sat impatiently while the women finished their meal. He cleared the table and said to Marie, "We can get those when we return." Marie just smiled at her loving husband.

He and Sasha led them down the street to the Milford house and it was difficult to determine which one was more excited. They walked the grounds and gardens of the house and then Theo opened the door and they stepped inside the lavish interior. The rooms were larger than they expected and the artisanship was impeccable. Hardwood floors graced each room and the walls were complemented by beautiful dentil trim work. Sasha and Milly fell in love with the place as they moved from room to room; leaving no doubt that this would be their next home.

Theo and Marie walked out to the porch, leaving Sasha and Milly alone to discuss their thoughts.

"What do you think, my love?" Sasha asked.

"I think we are home," Milly said as she turned toward Sasha. "This place is fabulous."

"I think it would be perfect for us," Sasha said, and Milly agreed.

"I don't think he would disagree, but let's ask Theo what he thinks about the place," Milly said as she reached for Sasha's hand.

They joined her parents on the porch and Sasha asked, "So what do you think?"

Marie looked at Theo and nodded her head. "We think this place would be perfect for the both of you," Theo said.

"We agree," Milly said.

Theo handed the keys to Sasha. "Welcome to your new home. Mother and I have already purchased the home for you as our welcoming gift to you," Theo said to Milly and Sasha.

"Oh Father, you shouldn't have," Sasha said.

"We have and that's that. We can contact the owner on Monday and finish out the deal," he said with a grin.

Sasha locked the door to what would soon be their new home and then joined Milly and her parents on the sidewalk. They returned to the Thibodaux's house and parted ways.

"I want to show Milly around for a while," Sasha said.

"Will you be back in time for lunch?" Marie asked.

"I think so, Mother," Sasha answered and then hugged them. "We won't be away for long." She turned to lead Milly down the walk.

Theo watched until they disappeared from view and then entered the house to help Marie clean up the kitchen.

†

Sasha was so excited to show Milly around their new hometown. They walked down to the harbor, and she showed Milly their office, and they walked for a while along the levee. As the morning burned away, Sasha led Milly to the cemetery. They sat on the small bench beside her grandmother's crypt and Sasha told Milly what she knew of her grandmother. Sasha kissed the headstone and they continued their tour of the city before heading for home and the lunch that would be waiting for them.

They found Marie and Theo sipping tea in the garden, and Sasha poured them each a glass as they joined her parents. "Such a fascinating city," Milly said as she took the glass Sasha offered.

"It is growing into a jewel of the south," Theo said proudly.

"Have you taken Milly to Jackson Square yet?" Marie asked.

"Not yet, Mother, I thought we might stroll down that way later this afternoon," Sasha said.

"Jackson Square is where many of our local artists set up displays to sell their work and to paint while the tourists admire their work. You can find every type of painter, fortune-tellers, and musical artists there on any day," Marie explained.

"Sounds like a very interesting place indeed," she said.

"So many of our talented artists would starve if it weren't for the tourists who are drawn to the lure of the Big Easy and elect to take a piece of the bayou back with them in the form of artwork," Sasha explained.

"What is the Big Easy?" Milly asked as she cocked her head curiously.

Sasha chuckled and said, "The Big Easy is one of the nicknames given to New Orleans. The laid-back way of life and the almost continuous party atmosphere are to blame for the name."

"The Big Easy," Milly said. "I like that."

Marie disappeared into the house and returned with a large plate of sandwiches, which she set on the table. "I hope you girls walked up an appetite," she said as she handed each of them a small plate.

"I do believe we did, Mother," Sasha said as she loaded a plate for Milly and herself.

"Why don't you take the coming week off from work to get settled into your new place," Theo suggested.

"That is an excellent suggestion, Theo," Marie said.

"Are you sure you wouldn't mind?" Sasha asked.

"Not at all, with your help we are actually ahead of schedule," Theo said to his daughter.

"Very well then. It looks like you are stuck with me for a week," she said to a grinning Milly.

"I think I can keep you busy for at least a week setting up house," Milly said.

†

They relaxed in the garden for an hour or more until Theo announced, "I think I will take a nap."

"We will go explore some more while you nap then, Father," Sasha said. "Would it be possible for Milly and I to treat you and Mother to a dinner in the Quarter tonight?"

"That would be great," Theo and Marie both said. "There is a new restaurant which serves fantastic Cajun dishes and has the most delightful bread pudding for dessert. Makes my mouth water just thinking about it," Theo said with a laugh.

"How about seven o'clock then?" Sasha asked.

"Seven will be perfect," Theo said and he retired for the afternoon.

"What plans have you for the afternoon, Mother?" Sasha asked.

"I think I will join your father for a nap," she said with a coy smile.

Sasha chuckled. "We will see you later this evening then," Sasha said as she took Milly's hand and left the house.

"You are fortunate to have such loving parents," Milly said as they strolled.

"Yes, I have been blessed to have them, and now you, in my life," Sasha said.

Sasha and Milly strolled down to Jackson Square and admired the artwork of many artists who had turned out on such a lovely day. As they approached a fortune-teller's booth, Sasha felt the now-familiar tingle of another immortal. The man who sat reading the palm of a lovely young tourist paused in his reading to look up and smile at them as they passed.

Greetings our brother, Milly sent their message.

Welcome sisters, he answered and then turned his attention back to the young woman.

"I have sensed several immortals here since my return," Sasha said.

"I imagine a city called the Big Easy would be an excellent place for our kind to live and hunt," Milly said.

"Would you care for a riding tour of the city?" Sasha asked as a mule-drawn carriage pulled up alongside of the curb.

"That would be lovely," she answered.

"Well, good day, Miss Thibodaux," the young driver said.

Sasha looked at the young man curiously, but could not place where she knew him.

The man chuckled and said, "The last time you saw me I barely reached your waist. It is James, Caroline's son, at your service."

Sasha finally realized that James was the son of Caroline Dupont, one of her mother's closest friends. "Oh my goodness, James, you have grown into such a tall and handsome young man," Sasha said.

"Well, it has been a few years, Sasha." He laughed. "Who is your beautiful companion?" he asked.

"I am sorry. James, this is Milly, my friend," Sasha said.

"Pleased to meet you, James," Milly said.

"Likewise, ma'am, and welcome to the Big Easy," he answered as he jumped down to the curb to assist them into the carriage.

Sasha reached into her purse to pay James for the tour, and he chuckled. "That will not be necessary, Sasha, this one is on me."

"Well, thank you, James," Sasha said. "How is your mother?"

"She is doing well, thank you. I will let her know you are back in town. I am sure she will want to visit," he said as he climbed back into the driver's seat.

For the next half hour, James entertained Milly and Sasha as he shared the history of the Big Easy with them and drove the many avenues of New Orleans. They covered much of the city during the tour, and Sasha asked if he could drop them off in the Garden District at the end of the tour.

"I am off for the evening and headed that way, so it would be my pleasure," James assured them.

He drove them to the heart of the Garden District and pulled over to the curb. "Are you sure I can't pay you for the ride?" Sasha asked.

"Heavens no, Sasha, not after all your family has done for mine. It is a pleasure to repay a little of your kindness," he said as he tipped his hat and pulled away from the curb.

"Charming fellow," Milly said as they watched James drive away.

They walked home together from the Garden District and then later that evening shared a wonderful meal with her parents.

✝

The following Monday, they settled the deal on the Milford house and spent the week setting up home. Their first purchase was a heavy four-poster bed with a thick goose down mattress, delivered for their first night in their new home. Together they bought other furnishings and by the end of the week, they had a respectable-looking home.

On Saturday, they invited Sasha's parents over for dinner, and Sasha prepared the pork roast and roasted vegetables using Ella's recipe. Theo ate several portions and raved to his daughter about how good the meal had been. Both Theo and Marie were impressed with how quickly they had been able to furnish and make the house feel like home.

"Don't you remember the fifteen trunks you had stored for us, Theo?" Milly teased.

"Ah, thanks for reminding me. I now have a warehouse again," Theo tossed back and they shared a hearty laugh.

They cleaned up the kitchen and then shared coffee out on the front porch where they watched a brilliant moon rising. "This weather has been too perfect so far," Theo said. "I hope this doesn't mean we will really have a hot, dry summer."

"Oh, and by the way, Robert from the office has been drafted and will be going off to join the army in the next few weeks. If you have a mind to join the shipping business, Milly, you are more than welcome to join us," Theo offered.

"I appreciate the offer, Theo, but I think it is best I stay out of the business world. I will be teaching at Tulane in the fall, thanks to your recommendation, but will be happy to assist you anyway I can over the summer," Milly said.

"Excellent idea, Milly," Marie said. "Let those two handle the business and enjoy your free time this summer."

"Free time," Sasha chuckled. "Mother, she already has plans for at least a dozen paintings and she just got here," she said.

135

Milly blushed slightly. "Well, there is much here that deserves to be painted," Milly said.

"I can't wait to see what you create," Marie said with genuine interest.

They continued talking and rocking until Theo started to doze. "I had better get your father home before he falls asleep in that chair," Marie said.

With a soft tap on Theo's shoulder she said, "Time to go home, Theo."

Theo startled and jumped in the chair. The three women laughed at his expression when he realized he had fallen asleep.

"Goodnight, Mother and Father," Sasha said as she hugged and kissed them. "I will see you in the office Monday," she said as Theo stepped off the porch.

"Stop in when you can," Marie said to Milly.

"I am sure you will see me next week as well," Milly said as she hugged her goodnight.

They watched Theo and Marie disappear into the night and returned inside the house eager to turn in for the evening. They stretched out comfortably on the thick mattress where they shared hours of tender kisses and caresses before entwining their bodies in blissful sleep.

Chapter Sixteen

The Storm of the Century

As summer waned and the Dog Days began, the heat and humidity in New Orleans was nearly unbearable. Tempers flared easily and people scurried to get indoors as quickly as possible to strip down to the bare necessities, and if they were fortunate enough to have a motorized fan, they found themselves perched in front of it.

The blood-red skies in the early morning were a portent, a warning that bad weather would soon be on its way. Theo scowled when he looked at the skies and arranged to prepare the warehouse for an imminent storm. Residents of New Orleans, all too familiar with tropical storms and hurricanes, took heed of their potential devastation. Nonperishable goods quickly left the shelves of the general stores and many a resident evacuated further inland to higher and drier locations.

"Sasha, I have a bad feeling about this storm," Theo said as they walked to the warehouse. People scurried about the streets, rushing to finish last-minute errands.

"What worries you so, Father?" Sasha asked.

"Just something down in my bones, makes me feel this will be a bad storm."

"Are there any other precautions we need to take, Father?" she asked.

"I think we are as prepared as we can be, but still…"

Reaching the warehouse Theo and Sasha closed the remaining storm shutters as workers raised the stored goods off the floor onto raised platforms in case of flooding. The heavy rains had commenced and Theo asked Sasha, "Please go ahead of me and help your mother with the shutters at our home. Then go as quickly as you can to your and Milly's home to ensure you are prepared for the storm." Theo felt Sasha's reluctance to leave him. "I will finish up here and rush home as quickly as I can," Theo said.

Sasha hesitated, preferring to wait for Theo. "Go please, Sasha," Theo said. He was concerned that Marie needed Sasha's help to secure the shutters.

Sasha hugged her father tightly and said, "Make it quick, it is getting wicked out there."

"I won't be far behind you, Sasha, so go," Theo said as he held the door open and they rushed out into the storm.

✝

Sasha watched as Theo made it to the office while waves crashed against the levee, sending a huge wall of spray flying through the air to mix with the pouring rain. She shielded her eyes from the rain as best she could and made a dash for her parents' home. The gusting wind pushed her backward as she struggled to run down the avenue, dodging flying tree limbs and debris. Sasha ducked a second too slow and a branch caught her across the cheekbone. She could feel her cheek swelling and the blood seeping from the open wound, the salt from her perspiration burning in the cut as the rain lashed at her face. Sasha ran as hard as she could, struggling to push forward into the strong wind, and when she was within two blocks of her parents' home the visibility was zero. She could not see the house for the driving rain, but she struggled on.

As she made it closer, she could see Marie on the front porch, struggling mightily against the wind as she tried to close a shutter. For every inch of headway she made, the wind pushed the small woman back six. Sasha rushed to her side and together they managed to fasten the shutter. She examined Marie's hard work, and found there were only two more left to secure the entire house. Sasha and Marie worked together to latch the last two shutters and then fought their way through the heavy front door. They collapsed against it, chests heaving as they struggled to catch their breaths.

"Thanks for your help," Marie said. "Where is your father?"

"He was securing the office and will be home shortly. Will you be all right until he gets here?" Sasha asked, worried about Milly and their home.

"Yes, Sasha. Go to Milly, and take care of your home," Marie said. "And have Milly take care of the cut on your cheek." She lovingly touched her daughter's swollen face. "When the storm breaks, we will stop by to check on you."

Sasha hugged and kissed her mother and then helped her close the door behind her before she ran out into the rain again. She was soaked to the bone and chilled as she ran as fast as she could to their home. Milly was on the porch with one shutter to go. Sasha ran up the steps and closed the shutter as Milly secured the latch. She turned and Sasha could see the wild look of fear in her lover's eyes, before she embraced Milly.

"Let's get inside and get out of these wet clothes," Sasha said as she led Milly to the door. She closed the door behind them, took Milly into the bedroom, and stripped the soaked clothes from her body. Milly was shivering with cold and fright as Sasha bundled her up in a thick robe.

"I am so afraid," Milly said as Sasha stripped off her own clothing and reached for a towel. Milly noticed the blood trickling down Sasha's cheek and the angry swollen flesh under her eye. "Oh no, Sasha, you are bleeding," Milly said as she rushed to her.

"It is just a small cut," Sasha said as she pressed the towel to her cheek to stop the bleeding. Sasha felt her immortal powers of regeneration at work and removed the towel to find the cut had already begun to heal.

"Everything will be all right," Sasha said as she tied the belt of the robe around her waist then reached for Milly. "I had forgotten that you have never experienced a hurricane, my love."

"What will happen to us?" Milly asked with a trembling lower lip.

Sasha wrapped her arms around Milly to comfort her lover. "The heavy rains will pound the earth for hours," Sasha said. "The winds will whip around and batter the house, sounding like a howling banshee. There will be severe damage to trees and homes around the area, especially those that aren't well protected, and some may lose their entire roof." Sasha stroked Milly's hair, soothing her terrified lover. "Our home is well protected and well elevated by New Orleans standards, so we should not be affected by flooding." A large gust of wind whooshed through the front porch. "Normally, the greatest danger is the cyclones that are spawned around the fringes of the storm. The cyclones spiral down from the sky to destroy everything in its path, but I think we will be taking this storm head on from all indications so far."

"Are we safe?" Milly asked.

"As much as we can be," Sasha said. "The weather will be frighteningly fierce for anywhere from eight to twelve hours until the storm passes over and heads inland and begins to die down." Sasha did her best to reassure Milly of their safety, but she silently worried that the storm would ravage her beloved city if it continued to strengthen. "Why don't we dress in some warm, dry clothes and get a hearty meal in our stomachs and then snuggle up together on the couch," Sasha suggested.

They dressed and moved downstairs to the kitchen. Sasha lit several hurricane lamps and placed them around as the shutters had left the room completely dark. She glanced at the clock to find that it was just after noon and walked to the front door to peer through one of the small glass panes as Milly toiled in the kitchen, preparing sandwiches, cheese wedges, and fruit sections, placing them on a small tray with a bottle of wine. When Sasha looked out the window the day had disappeared completely, and it was as black as midnight outside. She could not see beyond the edge of the porch until lightning flashed, illuminating the swaying trees. Sasha knew the storm would be moving inland soon.

She joined Milly on the couch and they shared the meal she had prepared. Sasha listened as the pelting hail came thundering down on the tin roof and shuddered when she heard the sound of a train whistle in the distance. She knew then that some part of the city was experiencing the rage of a cyclone, and she prayed for her fellow citizens.

Sasha watched as the flickering flame from the candle danced in Milly's wide eyes as she looked to Sasha for protection. Sasha took the remainder of the meal back into the kitchen and, picking up a thick quilt, returned to the couch. She stretched out the length of the couch, took Milly in her arms, and covered her with the quilt. "I will protect you, my love," Sasha whispered softly.

Sasha held on tightly to Milly who trembled and startled with each new onslaught of wind and rain against the house. "It is okay, Milly," Sasha calmly said, even though in her heart she knew they were in grave danger.

The interior of their home had grown silent as they listened to the wind shriek around the house. Whenever they heard a loud crack, or crash, Sasha knew a branch or entire tree had become a victim of the strong winds. The rain was the heaviest Sasha had ever experienced and she prayed the levee would be strong enough to hold back the flooding Big Muddy. She knew the city of New Orleans was in the shape of a large bowl, and was well below sea level. Even a minor storm brewed in the tropics could cause severe flooding in the downtown area, and Sasha hoped the heavier rains would pass through quickly. She softly stroked Milly's hair as she silently prayed for her friends and neighbors.

Two hours later, the wind and rains began to calm down as the eye of the storm approached. Milly noticed the change and thought the storm was over. "Is it over?" she asked timidly.

"Not yet, my love, the eye of the storm is approaching and the weather will return to almost normal for an hour or two as it passes over, but then we will receive the backside of the storm, which will continue for several more hours."

Milly, disheartened by this news, slumped back onto Sasha's chest. They could see through the front door's little window that it was becoming lighter outside. Sasha had lifted Milly to a sitting position so she could go and take a look outside when a loud pounding on the door started.

Sasha rushed to the door and pulled it open to find her mother standing there, soaked to the bone and tears pouring down her cheeks. She ushered her inside and closed the door behind them.

"What is wrong, Mother?" she asked.

"Theo hasn't made it home yet," Marie cried through her tears.

"What do you mean? He should have been there shortly after I left you," Sasha declared.

"I know, and I waited for him, but there has been no sign of him. Sasha, will you please go see if you can find him?" Marie implored of her daughter.

"Of course I will, Mother," she answered. "Milly, will you go with Mother back to their house and stay with her until we return?"

Milly was already on her feet before Sasha finished her request. She wrapped her arm around Marie's shoulder and walked her toward the door. Sasha walked with them back to her parents' home and saw them safely inside before beginning her search for Theo.

"Be careful, Sasha," Milly said as they parted.

"I will be back soon," Sasha said as she stepped off the porch and headed down the sidewalk.

Milly took Marie to the bedroom and helped her change into dry clothes and then they returned to the parlor to wait. Marie was in the beginning stages of shock, so Milly covered her with a warm quilt and sat beside Marie holding her hand. They sat together in silence, waiting for the ones they loved to return.

Chapter Seventeen

The Wrath of Nature

Sasha made her way down the avenue toward their office. The echoes of tin roof sections flapping in the wind broke the eerie stillness, while debris from trees and shattered homes was everywhere. She witnessed the devastation of several large oaks that had previously lined the avenue, ripped up by their roots and now lying across the street, creating an obstacle for Sasha to climb over or under to continue her search.

There was no sign of life as she walked. People had either chosen to evacuate, or were barricaded in their homes and not brave enough to venture out to assess the damage. She too, would still be bundled on the couch with Milly if her father were not missing. She tried reaching out with her mind to find Theo, but blackness was all she could feel.

She reached the warehouse and the structure looked sound. There were broken limbs surrounding it, but the building itself remained intact and free of damages. Sasha called out for Theo, but there was no answer. Only her voice echoed in the unnatural stillness. She walked on toward the office and unlocked the door when she arrived, but still no sign of her father. She was relieved the office was in good shape, but her concern for Theo was mounting quickly.

She began walking back toward her parents' home and decided to see if anyone was still at home at any of the several homes along the route her father would have taken.

At her first stop, the home of Mrs. Bronson, a widow in her late sixties, Sasha was welcomed at the door. "Hello, Sasha, my dear," the woman said. "Please be quick and come inside."

"I can't Mrs. Bronson, have you seen my father?" Sasha asked. "He never showed up at home."

"I did in fact see Theo. Your father stopped by to check on me just as he always has before a storm, and he braced my back door for me," Mrs. Bronson said with a worried look on her face. "He left here after about ten minutes. I sure hope Theo is safe. Please let me know when you find him."

"I will, Mrs. Bronson, and thank you for the information," Sasha said.

"Good luck my dear," the woman said and then closed the door.

Sasha stepped back onto the sidewalk and noted that the skies were beginning to darken again. She had to find Theo and soon so they could shelter from the backside of the storm.

Sasha visited two more homes and discovered that he had stopped by each to check on the occupants before continuing on his way. It was so like her father to make sure that his friends and neighbors were safe, Sasha thought as she continued her search. There was one more home Sasha was sure her father would have stopped by to check. His clerk, Robert, who was now in Europe fighting the war, lived just down the street. Theo would have stopped in to make sure Robert's wife and two children were safe.

Sasha stepped over a large oak branch that had landed on the sidewalk and noticed a faint red tint to the puddle of water, but it did not connect in her mind that the tint could be blood. She walked onto the porch and knocked on the door. Robert's wife Elizabeth opened the door and burst into tears as she saw Sasha standing there.

"Oh Sasha," she cried. "I am so sorry for what has happened." Barely able to form words Elizabeth fell into Sasha's arms.

Sasha looked beyond Elizabeth to see her two small children sitting on the floor playing quietly, and then shifted her gaze slightly to see her father lying on the couch.

"Father," Sasha whispered as she rushed into the house. She ran to his side and knew immediately that her father was dead. Sasha fell to her knees and took Theo's cold hand in hers. She burst into tears and looked up to Elizabeth for an answer as to what had happened to her father.

"Theo stopped by to check on us and make sure I had all the shutters in place, and as he was leaving, a large branch was torn off the old oak in the yard and struck Theo in the neck." Elizabeth was crying again. "The storm was raging violently, and with my children's help, I was able to bring him inside, but he never woke again," she said. "I couldn't leave the children during the storm, so I prayed that someone would be out once the eye passed over and could send a message to Marie for me."

Sasha stared in disbelief. Her father couldn't be dead.

"I just wish it would have been someone besides you, Sasha, I know how much you love your father," she said as she placed her hand on Sasha's shoulder. "I am so sorry."

"Oh Father," she softly cried. Sasha brushed the hair back from Theo's face and knew from the way his neck shifted that the blow had broken his neck instantly. At least he didn't suffer, she thought as she caressed his cheek.

"I will find some help and we will take him home," Sasha said as she left the house, feeling the shock beginning to set in.

Two houses down was the Smythe family. Sasha knew the couple had a strapping young son, and with luck, he and his father would be at home. She hammered on the door and the senior Mr. Smythe opened it quickly.

"Miss Thibodaux," he said. "Is everything all right?"

"No, Mr. Smythe," she answered on the verge of tears. "There has been an accident, and my father is dead. Would you and your son help me take him home?"

"Certainly we will," Mr. Smythe said as he called for his son.

"Father is next door on Elizabeth's couch. Could you go there and carry him home while I go break the news to Mother?" she asked.

"Yes, we will give you a few minutes head start and then we will follow you shortly," he said. "I am so sorry to hear this news. Theo was a great man."

"Thank you, Mr. Smythe, for your assistance and your words of comfort," Sasha said as she turned away and walked the short distance to her parents' home in a daze.

Milly jumped to her feet when she heard the front door open and rushed to meet Sasha.

Father is dead, Sasha projected to her lover and continued walking until she reached her mother and sat beside her.

Marie could tell by the horrified look on Sasha's face that something terrible had happened.

Sasha looked into her face, tears flowing down her cheeks. "Mother, there has been an accident and Father is dead," Sasha said. She could find no words to deliver the devastating news to her mother.

"Oh my God, no! Not Theo!" Marie cried as she collapsed in Sasha's arms.

Milly and Sasha sat beside Marie and held her as her body wracked with tears. *I am so sorry, my love,* Milly silently said.

As Marie's tears began to subside, Sasha sat her back on the couch. "Father stopped by to check on each of his neighbors on his way home. When he was checking on Elizabeth and the children, a large branch broke and struck Father in the neck," Sasha explained. "Mr. Smythe and his son will be here in a few minutes as I asked them to bring Father here for us."

"That was good of them. Should we place him on the couch until the storm passes and the mortuary can be contacted?" she asked for their advice, desperately trying to remain calm.

"I think that would be best," Sasha said and helped her mother cover the couch with a thick quilt as Milly crossed the room to answer the knocking at the door.

She opened the door and watched as the two men gently carried Theo inside and placed him on the couch. Mr. Smythe hugged Marie and said, "If we can do anything, just let us know," and then they left the house to give the family time alone.

Marie pulled an armchair up next to the couch and sat next to her beloved husband. She held his hand as she cried for his loss.

Milly moved over to Sasha and placed a protective arm around her. "Is there anything we can do for her?" she softly asked.

"Why don't you put a pot of water on for some hot tea," Sasha suggested. "This is going to be a long night ahead of us."

Milly went into the kitchen as Sasha watched her mother while she mourned the loss of her mate.

Just a few months ago, when she thought Milly had perished, Sasha had felt the same anguish her mother was now feeling. She knew there were no words of comfort during this time.

Milly made them a pot of tea and joined them in the parlor. The backside of the storm had arrived, battering the outside of the house with winds and rain as the flood of Marie's tears continued down her cheeks.

They sat with Marie during her deathbed vigil all night. She refused to try to get any sleep, preferring instead to spend her last hours with her beloved Theo.

When the storm ended shortly after midnight, Sasha walked outside to survey the storm damage and get some fresh air.

I will be back in a few minutes, Sasha projected to Milly.

Be careful my love, Milly answered.

Sasha opened the shutters on the front porch and stepped into the deathly quiet night. The winds that had raged for hours had turned into a soft breeze and the night sky was again visible, blanketed by thousands of stars. She circled the house, unable to detect any damage and walked the short distance to her and Milly's home. Except for some torn tree limbs, her home and gardens had fared well against the storm. Sasha sat down numbly on her front steps. As she stared up at the heavens, Sasha began to cry for her father, who had been her pillar of strength, throughout her entire life. She allowed herself to cry for several minutes then forced her tears back. Now more than ever, Marie would need her, and Sasha vowed she would be strong for her mother.

Sasha walked back to her parents' home and when she entered the house, she could hear Milly busy in the kitchen as she inventoried Marie's pantry. "I thought I would make us all some flapjacks and bacon," she said.

"I don't know whether we can persuade Mother to eat, but we can try," Sasha said as she kissed her lover's neck.

Milly turned in Sasha's arms and looked past her bruised cheek into her beautiful lavender eyes.

"How are you doing, my love?" she asked.

"My heart aches from our loss, but I know I must be strong for Mother," Sasha said.

Milly got Marie to eat a small portion of breakfast and drink a cup of coffee, which surprised them. At nearly five the next morning, Marie was near collapse from the emotional trauma. Sasha moved a small love seat next to the couch and laid her mother down beside Theo. Marie was exhausted, but fought sleep for as long as she could keep her eyes open, until finally sleep overtook her wearied body. Sasha covered her with a quilt and they watched over her as she slept.

Chapter Eighteen

Gone Home

When the clock in the foyer struck seven, Sasha stood and quietly led Milly from the parlor. "I need to go down to the mortuary and make arrangements for Father," she said. "I know there will be a great need for funeral services over the next week, and I want to be there early to take care of our business first. I will be back as soon as I can." With a soft kiss, Sasha left the house.

Sasha walked downtown, past the ruins of several buildings that had suffered severe damage. She was surprised that the avenues remained empty after the storm had passed, but she was on a mission to arrange for Theo's funeral, and could not be concerned with the state of her city.

When she entered the mortuary, Mr. Parker, who owned the business, met her. "Hello, Sasha," he said. "What can I do for you this morning?"

"Hello, Mr. Parker. Father was killed in a freak accident during the storm, and I need to make arrangements for his services," she said after greeting the soft-spoken man.

"I am so sorry to hear that, Sasha. Please pass my condolences to your mother as well. Now, Theo had already arranged and paid for services for him and Marie some years ago, so the arrangements will be uncomplicated," Mr. Parker said, much to Sasha's relief.

"Of course Father would have planned ahead," Sasha said proudly.

"Your father was a brilliant man and well organized. I just need to know where to pick him up, and when you would like the services to be held," Mr. Parker said. "Theo requested a traditional jazz funeral with the service performed by Father McCready at the gravesite."

"Father is in the parlor at home, and I think a service this Thursday would be appropriate," Sasha managed to say.

"Very well then, I will make all the final arrangements and send out the notifications. Go home and take care of your mother and yourself, Sasha," he said in a fatherly tone as he walked her to the door. "I will have the carriage come by as early as possible to collect your father, and he will be prepared for a wake tomorrow night." Mr. Parker held the door open for Sasha.

"Thank you, Mr. Parker," she said.

"My pleasure, just let me know if there is anything you need," he added.

Sasha walked outside into a bright, sunny morning and let her feet guide her to the Lawton Cemetery. She kissed her grandmother's headstone and said, "Father will be joining you soon, if he hasn't already arrived." A blackbird cried out, startling Sasha and she turned at the sound. The noisy bird was perched atop a headstone on the crypt next to her grandmother. In all the years she had visited her grandmother's crypt, she had never taken notice of the one next to hers. She was startled to see the name Thibodaux already carved into its magnificent stone, and underneath were Theo's and Marie's names with the dates of their births.

Sasha's knees failed her and she sank to the small bench. "Oh, Father," she cried and let her tears begin to flow. How this could have happened to her father, Sasha wondered. Theo was such a kind and considerate person to everyone he met, she felt he deserved to live a long life. If only she had found him sooner, there may have been a chance, but Theo had been dead too long to be reborn. Even then, Sasha was not sure her father would have approved of that option, so she would have to be content with Theo's fate. The loss of her father would leave a gaping hole in her heart, never be filled by any other.

Sasha wiped her tears and started the walk home. The news of Theo's death had spread quickly. When she approached her parents' home, there was a black wreath hanging on the front door to symbolize that the family within had lost a loved one. Sasha walked onto the porch and entered the house to find Milly sitting in the parlor watching over her father.

"Welcome back, my love," she said when Sasha entered the room.

"Thank you for being here with me, Milly," Sasha said as she walked to her lover and sat beside her on the love seat. "Is mother still resting?"

"Yes, she is. I took her to her bedroom earlier. I checked on her a few minutes ago and she was resting quietly," Milly said.

†

"The men from the mortuary will be here soon to take Father away," Sasha said.

"How are you doing?" Milly asked, concerned for her love.

"I am doing fine," Sasha said.

Milly knew her heart was breaking, but would not push Sasha to talk about her loss until she was ready. A soft knock on the front door interrupted their conversation and Sasha walked to the door to open it. Two men from the mortuary entered the house carrying a small stretcher. They carefully laid Theo on it and covered his body with a shroud.

"Mr. Parker said your father will be ready for viewing by seven this evening," one of the young men said before they carried Theo outside and loaded him into the back of a small-enclosed funeral carriage.

Sasha and Milly stood on the porch as the men drove away, carrying Theo from his home for the last time. Milly slipped her arm around Sasha's waist and guided her back inside as the carriage drove off. Once inside the house, she took her hand, led Sasha into the kitchen, and sat her at the small breakfast nook. She poured them each a cup of strong coffee and joined Sasha at the table.

"What will happen now?" Milly asked.

"The funeral services have been arranged for Thursday," she said. "There will be a private family viewing at the mortuary tonight and then for the friends and family the next two nights." Sasha took a sip of her coffee and continued. "People will begin to stop in, bringing food and flowers and offer their condolences to Mother and me.

"Father had made all the arrangements in advance for a jazz funeral, and he will be laid to rest beside his mother. I never noticed it before, but his crypt is right beside hers," Sasha said.

"A jazz funeral, what is that?" Milly asked.

"Death in Bayou country is celebrated in much the same way as life. It is seen as a rebirth as the person fades from this life to go forth to begin another as they cross over," she explained. "A brass jazz band will assemble outside the mortuary and lead the procession to the cemetery, playing various slow songs such as a funeral dirge or old religious hymns born from the days of slavery." Sasha looked at Milly and found she was studying her curiously. "Once they reach the cemetery, the service will be held and the body interred in the crypt. After the service is complete the band will again lead the procession from the cemetery to the home of the deceased, but this time fast-paced upbeat jazz songs and hymns will be played." Sasha drank from her cup again and grinned at Milly. "A favorite is 'When the Saints Go Marching in', as it is played to celebrate the life of the one who has gone home."

"That sounds like quite a production," Milly said.

"It is very theatrical," Sasha said. "The band will be conducted by a leader in a solid black tuxedo, who will appear solemn as he leads the procession to the cemetery, but when they return he will be dancing lively in the streets and leading the second line of dancers, a group of funeral goers, who dance and sing in celebration of the passing."

"Very unique," Milly said.

"It is viewed as a final message from the one who has gone home to the ones left behind that time for mourning has ended and life begins anew," Sasha concluded her explanation.

†

Sasha stood to answer a knock on the front door, and the first of many visitors were ushered into the parlor. The Smythe family carried in a large baked ham, and Elizabeth and her children brought in fresh-baked rolls. A flock of others soon followed and the dining room table filled with food and desserts. Caroline, her mother's best friend, was among them.

"Where is she?" Caroline asked softly.

"Upstairs, resting," she answered.

Sasha excused herself to go with Caroline to check on her mother. Marie was sitting on the edge of the bed as she entered the room. "We have visitors, Mother, do you feel ready to receive them?" she asked.

Marie turned to find Caroline standing just inside the room. She rushed to her friend and hugged her tightly.

"I am so sorry about Theo," Caroline said.

Marie nodded as she stepped back from Caroline. "Thank you for coming."

"I will be here for as long as you need me."

Marie nodded and smoothed her hair, then walked over to the mirror. "I look hideous," she said.

"Nonsense, Mother, you are as beautiful as ever," Sasha said as she placed her arm around her mother's shoulder.

Marie turned in her arms and hugged her daughter closely. "I am so thankful you are here with me now, Sasha."

"I will never leave you again," Sasha promised as she hugged her mother tightly.

"Now, you look just fine," Sasha said as she and Caroline led her mother to the parlor.

The guests approached Marie, individually or in small groups, to offer their condolences to her and her daughter. Marie accepted their offerings with the true grace of a Southern woman, her eyes damp with tears which she refused to let flow. They received guests until late in the afternoon and then decided they would take a brief nap before preparing for the viewing later that evening.

Sasha was thankful Caroline had arrived in the early afternoon and volunteered to stay with Marie until after the funeral. She busied herself with putting away the food and ironing a dress for Marie. Sasha and Milly walked Marie to her room and then slipped quietly into Sasha's childhood room.

Milly wrapped her arms around Sasha and held her mate as her tears flowed freely behind closed doors. She kissed Sasha's forehead, and stroked her hair until, finally exhausted, Sasha fell asleep.

Chapter Nineteen

Life Without Theo

The next few days flew past in a blur of emotions. The funeral attended by hundreds of Theo's friends and business contacts was a joyous celebration for most. Marie had difficulty adjusting to Theo not being in the house and Sasha was worried for her mother. She suggested an offer be made to Caroline and her husband to move into the house to give her companionship and some help around the house. This arrangement worked out well for Caroline and her family, as the couple's own home had received damage during the storm.

Sasha also hired James part-time to care for the gardens at both homes and life began to move on. The fire that used to burn in Marie's eyes while Theo was alive extinguished when he passed, and Sasha feared it would never return.

Sasha stepped into Theo's position at the office and the business thrived. She negotiated contracts with the government to ship supplies and equipment to Europe to support the troops, and worked diligently to manage the business as Theo had taught her. Milly started teaching at the university in the fall and spent hours painting in the garden, many times with Marie watching over her shoulder. Milly's art was the only activity of interest to Marie.

She loved to sit and watch her paint and with a little encouragement, Marie would accompany Milly to Jackson Square. Once the city finished repairs after the storm, the tourists returned and business for the artists of New Orleans flourished. The violent winds had torn free many slate shingles, which artists recycled, using the black slate slabs for small canvases. The paintings quickly became a tourist favorite.

Marie would talk with potential customers, giving them the historic facts about the piece Milly painted, and often sold the paintings faster than Milly could get them dry. They made a good team, and Sasha was happy the two women she loved so dearly were becoming such close friends.

✝

Many nights when Sasha returned from the harbor, she would find them toiling together in the kitchen, creating dishes for Sasha to sample or baking something truly sinful. Sasha would smile when she saw them together and was a willing guinea pig for their creations. She would sit at the table and read the paper while they finished creating dinner, and then they would share the meal. Sasha would rave about this dish or that, making them beam with pride.

"So when are you two going to open a restaurant?" Sasha asked one evening as she sampled their latest creation, a spicy étouffée.

"You know, that doesn't sound like such a bad idea," Milly said as she grinned at Marie. "We could persuade Caroline to join us. We could name it the Three Sisters' Café."

Sasha looked at her mother and could see the gears of her imagination spinning as she considered what Milly was suggesting. Deep in her eyes, the fire Sasha loved to see in her mother's eyes was slowly igniting. "Do you really think it would work?" Marie asked Sasha.

"I think it would be a smashing success with the three of you working together," she said. "In fact, I know of a little place on Royal Street that would be a perfect location."

Marie's eyes shone for the first time since Theo's death. "Are you serious, Milly?" she asked.

"Very much so," Milly said as she stood to clear the dishes from the table.

"Sasha and I will get those, Milly," Marie said. "Go back to the house and see if Caroline can drop by for a chat with us, if you would."

"I will put some coffee on while you are gone," Sasha said as she kissed Milly's forehead.

"I will be back shortly then," Milly said as she left the kitchen.

Marie and Sasha had washed the dishes and were sitting at the table drinking coffee when Milly returned with Caroline.

"What is this fantastic idea Milly is rambling about?" Caroline said as she accepted a cup of coffee from Sasha.

"Sasha has suggested that we open a restaurant, and Milly and I would like to know whether you would be interested in being a partner with us," Marie said.

"Tell me more," Caroline said, giddy with excitement.

"Sasha says there is a space on Royal Street that would be a good location to open the Three Sisters' Café," Marie said.

"We could begin by serving breakfast and lunch to see how it goes at first," Milly said.

Sasha sat back and observed as the women discussed plans for starting up their business. She could hear their excitement as they discussed menus, décor, and equipment they would need to purchase. Milly glanced up at Sasha and smiled, knowing that she was just as excited about the prospects of a restaurant as they were.

They chatted deep into that evening, and within a month, the café was beginning to take shape. Marie and Milly financed the purchase of the equipment while Sasha oversaw the renovation of the building they had bought. Caroline developed the menus and arranged to buy food supplies from the local merchants.

†

They decided they would open for business on New Year's Day and serve Hopping John free to all customers who came by that day. As is the custom in the Deep South, Hopping John is a meal consisting of black-eyed peas served over boiled white rice and seasoned with pepper sauce. Chunks of sweet Vidalia onions, and corn bread are served to complement the meal. It is believed that the coming year will hold good fortune if this meal is consumed on New Year's Day. The women felt this menu was a way to launch their business with an omen of good fortune for the coming year.

Therefore, the year 1916 started with a bang and the Three Sisters' Café was a huge success. Over the year, the breakfast and lunch crowds grew to such extent that they bought the small building next door and added a small covered patio with an expanded dining room.

Marie buried herself in operating the business to keep her mind occupied during the day. Her heart still ached for Theo, though, when she retired for the evening to an empty bed. There would be no one else for Marie. Her one true love was Theo, and she would carry her love for him to her grave.

†

160

The next three years rolled along smoothly, until late fall of 1919, when the Spanish Flu Pandemic reached New Orleans. Marie was one of the many unfortunately infected with the virus, and after suffering for three days, her spirit left to join her beloved Theo. Sasha wept for her mother's passing, but she knew Marie was relieved to finally be joining her precious Theo in the afterlife.

Marie was just one of thousands who would die from the deadly outbreak and that would spur the beginning of a change in mindset for Sasha. With both parents now gone, and New Orleans becoming so crowded, Sasha was beginning to feel claustrophobic. She began to feel uncomfortable in the city that she had loved all her life.

One day when Sasha was on a short business trip, she learned about a sugar plantation just south of New Orleans that was for sale, and before returning to the city, she stopped to inquire about the property. The moment she stepped on the grounds, Sasha fell in love with Sugarland, and she was determined to persuade Milly to make this their new home.

†

Later that evening, after they had made love, Milly snuggled into her body. Sasha asked, "Milly, how would you feel about moving out of New Orleans?"

Milly sat up in shock that Sasha would even mention such a proposition, knowing how much she loved the Big Easy. "Why, darling, what's wrong?" she asked.

"Since Mother has gone, it just doesn't feel like home anymore," Sasha answered with tears in her eyes.

"Well, you should know by now, I will follow you anywhere you wish to go," Milly sweetly said.

"I looked at a sugar cane plantation today that I think you would love. It is not far from the city," Sasha said to her lover.

"Why don't we go look at it together then," Milly suggested with a smile.

"You really wouldn't mind?" Sasha asked.

"No, my love, I wouldn't," Milly answered. "Our lives have grown so busy with the café and the shipping business, that we don't take time to do the things we love together like we should. I would love to have more time to spend painting or listening to your music," she said as she kissed Sasha.

"We will rent a carriage tomorrow then and drive out to look it over," Sasha said. "I am sure Caroline and her husband would jump at the chance to buy our house, and my parents' home shouldn't be difficult to sell either. Mr. Smythe and his sons have been asking for years about buying Father's company. I am sure they would jump at the opportunity."

"Caroline can handle running the café alone if she hires another cook," Milly chimed in as she looked at Sasha. The sparkle of excitement was beginning to return to Sasha's lavender eyes as she talked about the plantation, and Milly knew this place was something Sasha really wanted.

"We can even break down and buy one of those new automobiles people are raving about, so we can still visit the city to sell your paintings and look in on Caroline," Sasha teased.

Sasha became silent as she thought about the many other possibilities their future held, and when Milly looked at her again, she had fallen asleep with a smile playing across her lips as she dreamed of Sugarland.

†

The following morning, she and Milly walked downtown to rent a carriage and drove across the river bridge several miles south of the city. Sasha had arranged for the broker to meet them out at the property and they arrived with enough time to look around a while before he arrived. The house was enormous and accompanied by several outbuildings and a large stable. Sasha would love to own a pair of horses for her and Milly to enjoy.

The broker arrived and showed the house to them. They fell in love with the large parlor and rooms encompassing the house. A smaller building that used to be slave quarters had been converted into a small guesthouse. He explained that the sale included five hundred acres of prime cane fields, which now leased annually to a private farmer at a handsome cost, would generate good revenue. Sasha was amazed at the cost of the property and, with a nod from Milly, agreed to purchase the property. The broker offered to meet them in the city the next day to begin the purchase transaction. As they drove back to New Orleans, they talked excitedly about their new adventure and made plans for moving out to Sugarland.

Chapter Twenty

Another Great Move

Milly and Sasha stopped by her parents' home to talk with Caroline regarding their decision. James was also there working in the garden. They were shocked to learn that Sasha and Milly would be leaving the city. They understood her reasoning, but still thought she would never again leave New Orleans.

"We will be less than ten miles away," Sasha said. "We have also decided to buy an automobile so we can be back here in a matter of minutes if we are needed. And we will still come into town to sell Milly's paintings in the Square, so you will see us frequently."

"You are going to learn to drive an automobile?" James asked with a chuckle.

"Well, yes James. Does that seem impossible to you?" Sasha asked.

He chuckled again. "Somehow I don't see you behind the wheel of one of those contraptions," he said. "I have a better idea." Sasha looked at James closely. "You said that the plantation had guest quarters, correct?"

"Yes, it does," she answered.

"Well, Martha and I are expecting our first child. I would love to accompany you to the new place to work the grounds, and Martha could keep the house and cook for us," James suggested.

Sasha looked at Milly who was beaming. They both loved James and Martha and would welcome them as part of their new home. Sasha then turned to look at Caroline. "How would you feel about us taking your only son and his family out of town?" she asked.

"You said only ten minutes by automobile?" Caroline asked.

"Maybe less, for someone who knows how to drive," James said with a snicker.

Caroline smiled. "I could think of no one else I would rather have watch over my rascal of a son," Caroline said. "But..."

"But what," James said, his snicker cut short by his mother's response.

"When the time grows near, you and Martha will move in with your father and me so I can deliver my first grandchild," Caroline said.

It was Sasha's turn to chuckle. "That sounds like a good plan to me, because I am sure James wouldn't want me to try to deliver a baby."

They all laughed at Sasha's comment and the shocked look on James's face. "Don't you think you should go talk this over with Martha?" Sasha asked.

"I am on my way," James said. "Will you be here much longer?"

"Probably another hour or so as there is still some business to discuss," Sasha said as James moved to the door.

"I will be back shortly then," he said and disappeared.

Turning to Caroline, Sasha said, "I know you and your husband are looking for a home. Milly and I would like to offer ours to you if you would like to buy it."

Caroline stared, astonished by Sasha's request. She would love to have their house, and she knew her husband would jump at the opportunity. She could barely speak, but said, "Yes, I am sure we would love it."

"We are also giving you sole ownership of the café," Milly said, "if you are worried about how you will be able to afford the house."

"That is not necessary," Caroline said. "You and Marie worked just as hard as I did on that business."

"It is our gift to you, and we know Mother would have approved," Sasha said. "You meant the world to her."

Caroline broke down in tears at the mention of Marie. They had become so much more than friends over the nearly thirty years they had known each other, and she realized just how much she missed her.

Sasha embraced Caroline and calmed her tears. "I will speak to Mr. Smythe about buying the business and contact a broker about selling this house," she said just as James came bursting back through the door.

"Martha wants to know when we are moving," James said with a huge grin.

"We will know soon, James," Sasha said. "Why don't you and I walk downtown in the morning and take a look at these automobiles."

"I will be ready as soon as the sun comes up," James said.

"Well, let's make it a little later than that," Sasha laughed. "How about nine instead?"

"I will be waiting on your doorstep," James said. "I am going home now to help Martha start the packing," he said and with a kiss to his mother, a hug for Sasha and Milly, he was gone again.

"Bring your husband by later tonight and we will make arrangements about the house then," Sasha said as she and Milly moved toward the door.

"Thank you for everything," Caroline said as tears welled up in her eyes again and she hugged Sasha.

"You were the best friend Mother ever had, Caroline, and you devoted so much of your life to her and our family," Sasha reminded her.

Caroline hugged Milly and Sasha then walked them out to the porch. She watched as they walked down the sidewalk toward the home that would soon be hers. She could barely wait for her husband to come in from the sugar mill so she could share the news.

As they walked, Sasha slipped her hand inside Milly's and smiled to herself. Life was good. "I love you so, Milly."

"I love you too, Sasha."

†

Milly prepared a late lunch and they made plans for the remainder of the day as they ate in the breakfast nook. Sasha planned to pay a visit to Mr. Smythe to discuss the sale of the business. Milly would arrange to have their furnishings packed and relocated to Sugarland. Several of their regular customers at the café had the means to move a large household, and she was certain they would be willing to take on the task of moving furnishings from both theirs, and Theo and Marie's home. Sugarland was large enough that all the furniture from both homes would easily fit with room left to spare.

†

Sasha kissed Milly and left to track down Mr. Smythe and to run a few errands. She found Smythe and his eldest son sitting out in the gardens and asked to speak with them. She was ushered to a seat and brought a glass of tea. Within an hour of her arrival, Sasha and the Smythes had come to an agreement on the purchase of the business in which both parties felt they were receiving a fair deal. They agreed that Mr. Smythe would meet Sasha at the lawyer's office later in the week to draft the agreement. When Mr. Smythe's son heard that Sasha was also planning to sell her parents' home he asked if she would be willing to sell it to him.

Shocked by how fast things were moving, Sasha grinned and said, "I am sure we can work out a deal."

The younger Smythe smiled broadly at Sasha. "I have promised my love Elizabeth that we would wed once I found a suitable home and your parents' home would be perfect for us," he said.

Sasha smiled as she thought of young love shared inside the walls of her parents' home once again. "As soon as I have a broker price the home, I will be getting back with you and we will make a deal," she said.

"Perfect," he said and left to go in search of his love.

Their plans were working out well so far but Sasha had one more surprise she wanted to arrange before returning home for the evening.

She left the Smythe house and walked downtown to the bank. She walked in and asked to speak to Mr. Johnson, the bank's owner, and the proud owner of a fine horse farm on the edge of town.

"Miss Thibodaux," he said as he walked toward her. "To what do I owe the pleasure of your visit?"

"I need to do some business with you," Sasha said. "Milly and I have purchased the Sugarland plantation, and I would like to buy a pair of horses from you."

"Well, why don't we take a ride out to the farm? I think I have just the pair you are looking for," he said as he walked Sasha to the door. Telling the manager he would return later, Mr. Johnson closed the door behind them and ushered Sasha to the curb, opening the door to a shiny black automobile.

Sasha climbed inside the vehicle and sat back as Mr. Johnson gave her the first automobile ride of her life. She watched as he shifted the gears and maneuvered them through the busy streets, thinking it didn't look as difficult as James had made it seem.

In a matter of minutes, they were traveling down the driveway to the farm, and Sasha saw horses grazing in the fields. Several of the younger foals galloped along the driveway racing the motorized vehicle, easily leaving the slower behemoth behind.

Mr. Johnson drove directly to the stable and quickly walked around to open the door for Sasha. She took his arm and he led her into the large building. The building housed approximately twenty stalls, each filled with gallant-looking steeds. "I have a pair of palominos that are a perfect match for each other," he said as they walked down the corridor. "They are both four year olds and come from excellent bloodlines," he added. When he reached the first stall, a warm muzzle met Sasha as a large stallion poked his head out to nuzzle her cheek.

"This is Zeus," Mr. Johnson said as he stroked the large horse's neck. "You won't find a better horse to ride than Zeus," he said proudly. "He is strong and sure-footed and as powerful as a Greek God," he said with a chuckle.

"You are beautiful, aren't you?" Sasha said as she stroked down the horse's face.

Mr. Johnson moved to the next stall and motioned for Sasha to follow. "This gorgeous creature is Hera and has the fire to live up to her name as well."

Sasha was amazed how identical the two horses were, and except for a slight difference in height and weight, they were indeed a matched pair. Mr. Johnson motioned for two handlers to take the horses out into the paddock so Sasha could get a better view of their magnificence. She watched as they haltered the pair and led them out to the exercise paddock on long leads.

They were beautiful creatures and Sasha knew as she watched them that they were the pair for them. Once they agreed on the purchase price, Sasha arranged for their delivery to Sugarland, their new home. Smiling broadly, she rode back to town with Mr. Johnson and issued a draft to pay for the horses, then walked home.

Chapter Twenty-one

On the Move

The next morning, Sasha walked to the front door at half past eight and looked out the window. Sure enough, James was sitting on the front steps. She opened the door and welcomed him inside. "You may as well have a cup of coffee with us before we go downtown," Sasha said with a grin as she led the young man inside.

James joined them at the table and quickly drank the cup of coffee Milly served him. It was clear he was excited about the purchase of an automobile and Sasha worried he hadn't slept all night. "How did the packing go last night?" Sasha asked.

"Very well," he said. "Several of Martha's friends came over and helped us late into the night."

"Could you and Martha plan to move out this week, and maybe hire some of her friends to get the house ready for us?" Sasha asked.

"We should be ready in another day or so, and I am sure her friends will jump at the chance to make some extra money," James said.

"Have Martha offer them twenty dollars to clean while she supervises then, James," Sasha said. "I also have several chores for you to take care of, but we will discuss those later."

James continued to fidget, so Milly said, "I think it is time for you two to go." James bolted for the door.

"Thanks for the coffee, Milly," he said, but she wasn't sure he even tasted the cup he drank.

James and Sasha walked quickly down the street, both excited about making the purchase. "I need you and Martha to be moved by Wednesday, if possible, James, because I have two horses being delivered by Mr. Johnson and I need for you to care for them," she said.

"Horses! This move is getting better by the minute," he said with a grin. "We will be ready to take delivery by Wednesday, I promise."

Sasha handed him a hundred dollars in cash. "After we part today, I want you to take the car and go down to the livery to buy the tack, feed, and other supplies you will need." Sasha reached back into her pocket and pulled out another fifty dollars. "You might also want to take Martha out to Sugarland to look around so you will have an idea of what type of supplies you will need to prepare the house."

When they reached the merchant where automobiles were available for sale, she and James marveled at the three models they had on hand. All were black and each model was slightly different from the other. They finally settled on a sedan with plenty of room to seat four, and asked the owner to take them out for a test drive. James eagerly slipped behind the wheel as Sasha took a backseat while the owner instructed James on driving the vehicle. With just a few false starts, James quickly got the hang of shifting the gears and they maneuvered around the city with ease. James was like a child at Christmas as he steered the sleek vehicle through the streets and headed toward Sasha's home. He parked on the curb and ran inside to get Milly, as Sasha had asked.

Milly joined them for the return ride downtown. After paying for the vehicle, Sasha said, "James, drive us out to Sugarland, please." She gave him instructions for the turns, and in fifteen minutes, they were rolling down the driveway to Sugarland.

"This place is fantastic," James said as he parked the car in the driveway.

They started in the main house, showed him the guesthouse where he and Martha would live, then walked through the stable. "Martha is going to love this place," he said with a wide grin.

"Be sure to bring her out today so she can see for herself," Sasha said as they returned to the automobile.

James drove past endless cane fields on his way back to town and made a note of each turn he would need to make to drive back out to the property. When the river came into sight, Sasha said, "Drop us by the house, and then we will see you tomorrow."

James dropped them at the curb and then drove to his home to collect Martha. He would stop by the livery to pick up the supplies Sasha requested then take Martha out to Sugarland.

"He is just like a child," Milly said as they watched him drive off.

"A very excited child." She chuckled. "Why don't we walk down to the café for some lunch," Sasha suggested.

"That sounds good. Maybe afterward we can come back here for some dessert?" she replied with a coy smile.

"Or we could just stay in and have dessert," Sasha said.

"It will wait," Milly said as she took Sasha's hand and together they walked downtown.

†

"Hello, ladies," Caroline said as they walked in the door to the café.

"Hello, Caroline," Milly said. "We were both missing your cooking, so we thought we would drop by for some lunch."

"We have a fantastic grouper with pecan sauce today or some red beans and rice, if you are looking for a touch more spice," she said.

"Let's try one of each," Sasha suggested as they walked over to a table by the window. "Has James stopped by yet?"

"He sure did and took me for a short ride in your new automobile. I don't care what anyone says about progress, I will stick to my own two feet or a horse-drawn carriage," Caroline said with a smile.

Sasha and Milly laughed at Caroline's declaration as she disappeared into the kitchen. She returned a moment later with glasses of tea for them and placed a small bowl of fried crawfish on the table between them with a bottle of hot sauce. "These should hold you over for a few minutes until your lunch arrives."

Milly opened the hot sauce and poured it over the crawfish before handing Sasha a fork. "Dig in, love," she said.

They ate the spicy crawfish and chatted with Caroline while they waited on their lunches to arrive. James had told his mother about the property and Caroline said she couldn't wait to see the place. "Well if you can survive another one of James's wild rides, maybe he could bring you out later in the week," Sasha said. "I hope we can have the furniture at least partly moved after Martha and her friends finish cleaning."

"James did say he and Martha would be moved by the day after tomorrow when he breezed through here. He is so excited, Sasha, and he can't wait to see your special purchase," she said without thinking.

"Special purchase," Milly said. "What special purchase?"

Sasha looked at Caroline and quickly shook her head.

"Well, I have no idea what he meant," Caroline said, trying to cover her error and then rushed away to the kitchen to check on their food.

Milly turned and looked at Sasha. "What have you got planned now, my darling?" she asked.

Sasha grinned and then simply said, "I have no idea what he is talking about."

Sasha could feel Milly trying to enter her mind and she chuckled. "That won't work either, my dear."

Caroline returned with their meals and left them to enjoy their lunch. They ate half of each entrée then exchanged plates. The food, of course, was fabulous and they raved about it to Caroline.

"That meal was fantastic," Sasha said as they prepared to leave the cafe.

Not nearly as tasty as dessert is going to be, Milly projected with a grin.

Sasha returned her grin. Am I guaranteed of seconds?

You're guaranteed anything you desire, my love, Milly said.

"That sounds very promising," Sasha said aloud as she closed the door behind them.

†

They walked quickly back to their home and Sasha disappeared into the bathroom to prepare water for a bath. Milly undressed in the bedroom and lit candles around the bed before joining Sasha in the bathroom, just as she poured the last of the hot water into the large claw-foot tub.

The sight of Milly naked as she walked toward her always made her heart race, and Sasha reached out to take her lover in her arms.

"Hello, beautiful," she said as she covered Milly's lips with her own.

As they kissed, Milly sat against the edge of the tub and allowed her hands to play up Sasha's sides. They ended the kiss, and Sasha shivered as Milly's fingers began manipulating the small buttons on her dress.

Sasha watched her lover closely as she undressed her, clothes falling into a pile on the bathroom floor. Milly leaned forward and her lips lightly kissed each of Sasha's hard nipples.

Sasha stepped into the tub and sat in the steamy water as Milly climbed in behind her and pulled Sasha back against her soft chest. Milly nuzzled in Sasha's neck as her hands lathered a soft bathing sponge with fragrant soap and she began to bathe her lover. Milly's hands moved across Sasha's breast with the lightest of touches as she caressed the soap across her skin. Sasha turned her head toward Milly and they kissed, softly at first and then more passionately as Milly's hands moved further down Sasha's body. Milly's right hand vanished beneath the water and moved to spread Sasha's thighs. Her fingers explored Sasha's lower lips until they located her swollen clit, stroking it lightly as it continued to swell. Her left hand had encircled Sasha's body and was kneading the soft mounds of her breasts, her fingers gently twisting the swollen nipples. Their tongues danced sensually, their moans of pleasure blending as Sasha reached her climax and shuddered in Milly's arms.

Milly removed her fingers slowly, finished bathing their bodies, and after drying them, led Sasha into their bedroom.

Chapter Twenty-two

As Time Flies

Milly laid Sasha down across the comfortable bed and stretched out beside her. Her hands softly stroked Sasha's face and lovingly stroked down her body. Sasha enjoyed the sensation of Milly's touch and watched as her lover explored her body like it was the first time again. Her body shivered with delight when Milly's fingertips brushed across her nipples; she moaned her pleasure as Milly teased her body with soft touches.

Sasha looked up to find Milly watching her with eyes that glowed with desire and felt her insides melt with arousal. She watched as Milly moved to sit between her legs and placed her hand on her right ankle. She lifted Sasha's leg in her hands and planted soft kisses, with gentle nibbles spaced between kisses, all the way up her thigh to the crease between her leg and trunk. When she reached Sasha's soft lips, Milly used her tongue to lick lightly above them, tasting the sweet nectar that was flowing freely from her body. Sasha's moans grew louder then stopped when Milly's tongue began to descend the opposite leg. The movement of Milly's mouth and hands was pure torture for Sasha, whose body was screaming for release. Milly raised her body to hover above Sasha, then lowered it to rest breast against breast, and wetness to wetness as her mouth covered Sasha's with a tender kiss. Sasha's hands caressed down Milly's back and pulled her hips firmly against hers as she began to roll her hips into Milly's body.

Milly kissed down Sasha's neck and her hands cupped her breasts, tenderly squeezing and kneading them. Milly continued kissing down her body and when her mouth covered Sasha's right breast, Sasha gasped at the intense pleasure she received from the tongue that was lazily circling her throbbing nipple. Sasha's body trembled with desire as Milly lowered her hand between them and entered her body with three fingers as their hips moved together. Sasha thrust her body against Milly, forcing her fingers deep inside, and after several minutes she was shuddering in climax.

Milly turned to straddle Sasha with her wetness positioned just above Sasha's eager tongue. She lowered her mouth onto Sasha's pulsing clit as her fingers continued to stroke in and out of her. Milly lowered her hips to allow Sasha's tongue to lick lightly down her lips, teasing her with the sultry taste of her body as she drank freely from Sasha. Sasha placed her hands on Milly's hips and pulled her down onto her mouth as her tongue explored deeply inside Milly's body, while her fingers twisted her aching nipples. Both lovers took great pleasure in one another's body and together they reached climax and lay trembling in a mass of entwined arms and legs.

Milly turned around and Sasha pulled her close, her arms encircling her body. She could hear the heartbeat in Sasha's chest, which matched her own strong rhythm beat for beat as she looked up into Sasha's eyes. "I love you," she whispered.

"I love you too," Sasha softly answered and her hand stroked the silky lengths of Milly's hair.

The two lovers dozed for the remainder of the evening and went out early the next morning to feed on prey that was stumbling home from a night of raucous partying on Bourbon Street.

†

The rest of that week sped past in a blur as the business and homes sold, and they were ready to move into Sugarland. James drove into the city to take them out to Sugarland once the last load of furniture had arrived and was arranged in the house. Sasha and Milly toured the home and were pleased with how the house had come together. Martha and James were toiling away preparing dinner when they reached the kitchen.

"Have you taken her to the stable yet?" James asked.

"Not yet, James, I think I will do that now," Sasha said. She took Milly by the hand, led her from the house, and toward the stable as James and Martha watched out the window.

Zeus and Hera poked their heads out of their stalls and whinnied to welcome them as Sasha and Milly entered.

"They are so beautiful," Milly said as Sasha made the introductions. "When can we ride?"

"I thought we could take them out for a long ride tomorrow and survey the property," Sasha said. "Maybe ask Martha to pack us a picnic lunch and spend the day riding."

"That sounds wonderful to me," Milly said as she leaned in to kiss Sasha.

They walked back to the house and sat in the kitchen as Martha finished preparing dinner.

"Aren't they beautiful?" James said when they returned to the house.

"They are wonderful, James," Milly said with a warm smile. "I can't wait to go riding."

They ate the meal and afterward Milly and Sasha retired to the parlor. Sasha had brought Marie's baby grand out and had it placed in the parlor. She ran her fingers along the cover and slowly opened it to reveal the shimmering white keys. Milly sat on the love seat and watched as Sasha sat on the bench and began to caress the keys. It had been months since Sasha had played and the keys were like heaven to her fingertips. Her rapture was evident on her face as she closed her eyes and began to play. Milly watched and fell in love with her all over again.

Later that evening, after Martha and James had retired, Milly took Sasha by the hand, and led her to the master bedroom to celebrate their first night in their new home. Their bodies entwined for hours and the sheets were soaked with the fruits of their lovemaking as they gave and received pleasure from one another. They finally slept only hours before the sun was due to rise, and when they awoke they bathed and dressed in riding clothes.

Martha was busy preparing breakfast of scrambled eggs, bacon, and fresh-baked biscuits, when Sasha and Milly arrived in the kitchen. She poured each of them a cup of coffee and carried it to the table. "I have a nice picnic packed for you ladies," Martha said as she pointed to the small bag Sasha would fasten to her saddle. "James is out in the stable now preparing the horses for your ride, but he will be in shortly." Martha placed fresh-baked biscuits, homemade butter, and honey on the table.

Sasha opened one of the still-steaming biscuits and covered it with a pat of fresh butter then poured honey over the melted butter. She picked up a half and bit into the sumptuous treat and moaned her pleasure loudly. "These are fantastic, Martha," Sasha said as she took the other half and offered it to Milly, who took a large bite.

"Mmm, you are so right, Sasha, these are the best I have ever tasted," she agreed.

Martha glowed with their praise as she dished up the eggs and carried them with the bacon over to the table. "I am glad you are pleased," she said as she sat at the table with them.

"Won't you join us?" Sasha asked.

"I will wait until James comes in and cook his eggs fresh," Martha said with a smile. The smile she wore made it apparent how deeply she loved James and the smile turned brighter when she heard him enter from the back porch.

"Good morning, ladies," James said as he walked over to Martha and kissed her forehead. "Those smell delicious," he said as he took a biscuit and coated it with butter and honey.

Martha stood and poured him a cup of coffee. "Get us a plate down, James, while I scramble more eggs," she instructed.

James took the last bite of his biscuit, walked to the cupboard to retrieve plates, and carried them to the table.

"The horses are saddled and ready to go when you are," he said to Sasha and Milly.

"Thank you, James," Sasha said as she bit into a slice of thick-cut bacon.

"You are welcome," he said as he watched Martha walk to the table with a large bowl of scrambled eggs. "You know, for a few dollars, I could set us up with a chicken coop and we could raise our own; and we could have fresh milk if we had a cow," James said. "While we are at it, I hope you don't mind, but I would also like to put in a small garden out back."

"Well, James, I do believe life in the country is good for you," Sasha said as she watched how excited he got while he discussed his plan. "Just let me know how much you need."

"I still have money left from the money you gave me for supplies and that should be an adequate amount." James grinned at Sasha as he dished out a large spoonful of the eggs and dug into the hearty meal.

Sasha and Milly finished their breakfast and left the house for the stables. James had saddled the horses and tied them at a hitching post before going back to the house. Sasha tied the small bag holding their lunch to her saddle horn and then walked over to help Milly mount Hera.

They walked the horses down the drive until they reached a cart road and turned left. Sasha and Milly passed endless fields of dense sugar cane, which would soon be ready for harvest. They had been riding for nearly half an hour when they rode up a small path. The horses instinctively followed the path with little guidance from their riders, who were busy looking at the surrounding woods. After a few minutes, the trees became less dense and a small clearing appeared. Nestled between large oaks was a cottage. Milly and Sasha approached the small building and after dismounting, walked onto the porch and through the front door.

The cottage was small inside with no interior walls. There was a small cot, a bare kitchen and a small table placed in front of the large window on the front of the house. The cottage was dark and it appeared no one had lived there for years. They examined it carefully and could see that the building appeared well maintained.

Milly looked around the cottage and then smiled warmly at Sasha. "Darling, would you mind if I made this my new studio?" she asked.

"No, in fact I was thinking the same thing," Sasha said. "With a little cleaning and some nice lamps, this could be an excellent place to paint."

"It isn't far from the house, either, so I could walk or ride Hera," Milly said.

"I will ask James to build a small corral where Hera can roam while you paint then," Sasha said. "I am sure he will jump to the task quickly.

"I can bring you lunch every day," Sasha added with a dreamy quality to her voice.

"Ah, I would love that," Milly said as she took Sasha in her arms. "We could have dessert too." Milly nodded to the small cot across the room.

Sasha smiled broadly at the mention of dessert. She would ask James to bring a small bed and ask Martha to send clean linens.

After they finished discussing plans for the cottage, they mounted the horses and continued their ride. They rode deeper into the dense forest until they found a small clearing, which had a freshwater spring that someone had harnessed in a large vat. A tin cup hung by its handle next to the vat. Sasha dismounted and took the cup and dipped it into the spring. The water was cold and refreshing as she sipped and then handed the cup to Milly. There was also a small trough at the base of the vat and a tap that when turned would fill the trough to water the horses. Sasha took the cup and returned it to its resting place. She opened the tap to fill the trough for the horses and then helped Milly down.

They found a flat clearing next to an old oak tree and opened the bag to find the lunch Martha had packed for them. Sasha opened a fold of waxed paper, which held slices of meat and cheeses, and another, which held slices of fresh bread. She made them sandwiches and then leaned back against the tree. Martha had also packed boiled eggs that they ate. Sasha went to the spring for a cup of the fresh water. She drank deeply and carried a cup to Milly.

They relaxed against the tree and looked out across the expanse of the bayou. Cypress grew in twisted forms, draped by thick strands of Spanish moss. The bayou was beautiful in the daylight; at nightfall the nocturnal creatures would come out to feed, and the bayou would come to life with their sounds. Sasha knew there would be many nights ahead that she and Milly would sit out on the porch in the swing or rocking chairs and watch the fireflies as they danced for their mates, and she smiled and placed her arm around Milly's shoulder.

Chapter Twenty-three

The Plantation

That was how life began at Sugarland. Sasha took daily rides around the property while Milly toiled away in her cottage studio to paint the morning away. As promised, Sasha brought her lunch while she painted, then many afternoons were shared on the small bed, as they loved the day away.

On the weekends, James or Sasha would drive them into the city and Milly would sell her paintings while Sasha visited friends or stopped by to look in on business at the café.

When they needed to feed, Sasha and Milly would scour the bayou for lone poachers, and it wasn't long before the story of the sirens of the bayou took form. Rumors told that the bayou was home to two beautiful sirens that would enchant men that ventured alone into the bayou at night. The survivors of the encounter would tell that they could only remember the beauty of the women and the intense pleasure of the kiss they would give their victims. They could not recall the description of the women so Milly and Sasha fed on their victims without fear of detection. On the rare occasion when they would take a life, the alligators of the bayou would consume the bodies of the dead who later were declared missing in the bayou.

†

James and Martha had a fruitful love life and they had four children over the next twenty years. The children grew up a part of Sugarland and returned often after they started families of their own to visit their extended family. Even as James and Martha began to show signs of aging, no one ever mentioned that Sasha and Milly continued to look young and vibrant. Blessed by a slow aging process, as a reward for their service to Milly and Sasha, even James and Martha looked much younger than their real ages. They jokingly referred to the fresh spring water they consumed as the fountain of youth and attributed their appearance to its magic water.

†

While in the city one weekend, Sasha visited Marcus, a French-born vampire who had made his way across the ocean to settle in New Orleans. They had become good friends over the past ten years and one Saturday morning in the late 1960s, he shared good news with Sasha.

"Have you heard of the Network, my friend?" he asked Sasha as they sipped on strong coffee down in the Quarter.

"The Network?" she asked. "What is it?"

"In Atlanta there is a small group of immortals who are working to develop a serum that can be used as a substitute to human blood," Marcus said, immediately piquing Sasha's interest. "So far they have been able to develop a formula that satisfies the hunger for almost a week in most subjects, but they are hopeful to one day create the perfect formula."

"That would make life so much easier," Sasha said. "Can you imagine walking to your refrigerator for a bottle of serum instead of hunting for your next meal?"

"It would be much safer for us," Marcus said. "Anyhow, I am going to order some of the serum and will order some for you and Milly if you are willing to be a part of the experiment."

"Count us in," Sasha said as she thought of a life where there would be no need to feed on humans any longer.

"I will, and I'll let you know when it arrives from Atlanta," he said with a smile.

"I have an idea, Marcus, and I would appreciate your opinion," Sasha said a few minutes later as she watched a group of tourists walk by as a tour guide lectured them on haunted New Orleans and the many ghosts and voodoo practices legendary to the city.

"Of course, my friend," Marcus said. "What is it?"

"I was thinking about converting Sugarland into a bed-and-breakfast bayou resort," she said, adding that she and Milly had become acquainted with the many specters that lived at Sugarland and cohabitated with them peacefully.

"With the increase in tourism in New Orleans I think a haunted plantation in the heart of the bayou would be attractive to tourists who wanted the nightlife and a little *lagniappe*," she said with a grin.

"I think that is a marvelous idea," Marcus said as he chuckled at the "little bit of extra" comment Sasha had made. "People are becoming obsessed with ghosts and UFOs. I doubt you would have any problems turning it into a thriving business."

Sasha agreed and decided to discuss the idea with Milly on their ride home later that evening. After visiting with Marcus, Sasha walked to the cemetery and placed fresh flowers in the vase on her parents' and grandmother's crypts. She missed her parents terribly, especially Theo, who had been not only her father but also one of her closest friends. Milly's words to her back in Europe rang in her ears as she recalled her saying that Sasha would watch her loved ones grow old and die, while she remained young for centuries. Her heart was weighted with sadness as Sasha realized how accurate her words had become.

Milly had just finished with the sale of a painting when she felt a wave of sadness. She reached out with her mind to locate Sasha and said, *My love, are you all right?*

Yes, dear one, I am visiting the cemetery, Sasha answered.

I see, Milly said. "I miss you, so hurry back to me.

I will see you soon, Sasha answered as she began her stroll back to the Square.

Tourism had helped New Orleans grow into the vivacious city it had become, but not without a cost to its beauty. The streets and avenues were littered with refuse, and the alleys smelled strongly of stale urine. Sasha sometimes missed the convenience of the city, but she was also happy to have the solitude of Sugarland to welcome her home. Sasha could hear one of the many brass bands that performed for tourists around the Square long before she could see them. The uplifting jazz tune they played improved her spirits and her pace quickened as she danced down the sidewalk to the beat of their music.

Milly saw her dancing down the sidewalk and smiled broadly at the woman she loved so completely. Sasha joined her and sat beside her to watch as she completed a painting on one of the solid black slates that had become so popular. A bayou scene full of twisted cypress covered with moss and inhabited by several large cranes came to life before her eyes. Milly leaned it against the wrought-iron fence surrounding the square to dry and leaned back in her chair to enjoy the sunshine. She had brought six completed canvases into town this morning and only one remained, besides the three slates she had completed that morning. She would remain in the Square for another hour and then treat Sasha to lunch in the Quarter before they left for home.

Sasha leaned back in her chair and propped her feet on the wall as she watched visitors walk or ride past in one of the many mule-drawn carriages that had grown so popular with the city's visitors. Her eyes had grown heavy and she was nearing sleep when Milly said, "Are you ready for some lunch?"

"I thought you would never ask," Sasha said.

"Let's go down to Ralph and Kacoos and have some crawfish," Milly suggested.

"That's a delicious idea," Sasha said as she drove them over to Toulouse Street and found a parking spot.

They each ordered crawfish tails for an appetizer and then étouffée, consisting of crawfish tails in a spicy roux served over white rice. Afterward, they shared a large serving of bread pudding and left the restaurant completely satisfied.

As she drove them home, Sasha asked, "How would you feel about using part of Sugarland as a bed-and-breakfast?"

"I think that is a great idea," Milly said. "With all the children gone, Martha doesn't have a crew to cook for anymore."

"She and James would probably welcome the extra work," Sasha said as she concentrated on the road. "I was thinking we could convert five of the lower level rooms into guest rooms and offer transportation into the city so our guests can enjoy the nightlife and what the city has to offer."

"Why don't we discuss it with them later tonight then," Milly suggested.

"That's fine with me," Sasha said as she turned the car into the drive, a broad smile playing across her face.

†

As they had expected, James and Martha were excited about the prospect of a bed-and-breakfast, so Sasha began drafting a business plan. James would resurface the hardwood floors and put a coat of fresh paint on the walls. Milly would paint several oil paintings for each room, while Martha developed menus for meals that she could prepare for their guests. Julia, their youngest daughter, was a student at Tulane and Martha was sure she would be willing to help with meal service and housekeeping on the weekends while she finished her studies.

She and Milly went back into New Orleans, bought a business license, and met with travel agencies and tour groups to begin advertising their new business. The travel agents were just as excited about the bed-and-breakfast idea and promised to send them as many referrals as possible.

They returned home that day pleased with their accomplishments and three weeks later were open for business. As promised, the travel agents sent customer referrals and for their first weekend, they had all five rooms filled. They were all pleased with how well the business had started, and visitors vowed to return on their next trip to New Orleans.

Meanwhile, Milly and Sasha had become accustomed to dosing with the Network's latest serum and they found they needed to hunt less frequently. A downside to the serum was, when they did feed, their hunger was great, and they took the lives of their victims. However, by hunting deep in the bayou and rarely venturing into the city, their activity remained undetected.

It was on one of those rare nights when they chose to hunt in the city that the trouble began. Sasha had parked the car down by the brewery, and they had walked through the dark alleys toward Bourbon Street. As they approached, a lone drunk came stumbling toward them, and they easily ushered him into the alley and began to feed. Neither of them had seen the homeless man, hunched in a doorway, as they passed, and they did not become aware of his presence until they began to feed and he went screeching back down the alley toward Bourbon Street.

"Finish this one and I will take care of the other," Milly said as she moved quickly after the frightened man. She quickly caught up to him and pulled him into the alley. They had made a huge mistake tonight, becoming complacent in their hunting techniques. Had the man remained quiet he would have survived this night; instead, he would forfeit his life to feed Milly and to protect their presence. Milly drank from him freely and then broke his neck, and set his body next to several empty liquor bottles. When his body was found in that condition the police would not take the time to investigate the death of an obvious homeless drunk.

Sasha had finished feeding on her victim and had discarded his body in a large construction Dumpster and covered it with debris to prevent detection. She too realized the error they had made that night, and that realization struck her like a bolt of lightning.

"We need to get out of here," Sasha said. "That was much too close for comfort."

"I am so sorry," Milly said.

"It is as much my fault as it is yours, Milly, but we must be more careful," Sasha said.

She and Milly hurried back to their car and silently rode back to Sugarland. When they returned home, they vowed to hunt in the bayou in the future as tonight's scare had struck too close to home.

Milly felt ill as she climbed into the bed, but quickly drifted off to sleep while Sasha stared at the ceiling and relived the night's terror over and over.

Chapter Twenty-four

Withering

Over the next three years, Sasha watched as Milly started to slowly decline. She grew increasingly lethargic, but nothing they tried would bring her back to normal. In October of 1980, Sasha persuaded Milly to travel to Baton Rouge to meet with a physician, who was also an immortal, to have some tests run to determine why her health was failing.

Sasha drove them to Baton Rouge, and they went immediately to see the physician. Dr. Moore welcomed them into his small office and began by drawing blood and performing a physical examination on Milly. His frown deepened as she described her symptoms to him and he hesitated to attempt a diagnosis before getting the test results.

"Unfortunately, I have seen these exact symptoms in several immortals in the last few years, and I fear I will be seeing more as the coming years pass," he said as he ushered them to his private office. "Mind you, the laboratory test results will take about a week, but I am confident I know what the problem is."

Sasha reached over and took Milly's hand, as she knew there was disturbing news to come.

"There is a new plague among humankind and unfortunately it is affecting immortals as well." Dr. Moore looked first at Sasha and then at Milly. "I assume you wish to know all the facts without the sugarcoating," he said.

"Yes, Doctor, tell us what we need to do," Sasha said.

"Unfortunately, Miss Thibodaux, nothing can be done," he said. "This new disease, called AIDS, attacks the immune system of humans, and is carried by their blood. When an immortal feeds on an infected human, they also contract the disease." He forced himself to smile at Milly. "The infection causes the immortal's body to lose its ability to regenerate."

Milly took a deep breath and asked, "What will happen next?"

"You have already described the lesions that appear and disappear after a day or two as your body's system regenerates itself," he said. He swallowed hard as he continued to speak. "This indicates that you have a full-blown case of the disease and have probably been infected for a few years. Your body will continue to slowly lose its ability to regenerate until one day you will fade from this life."

Tears rolled down Sasha's cheeks as she listened to the doctor's prognosis. Milly remained in a state of shock as she realized that she was dying and nothing could be changed to prevent that. The very blood she needed to sustain her life had proved to be her undoing.

"I wish I had more positive news to share, but I would say that given your symptoms, you may have six months to a year at best," he said.

"Is there nothing that can be done?" Sasha managed to ask.

"I am afraid not. The virus has mutated several times, and our attempts to create a vaccine and treatment for the disease have proven futile." He shifted papers on his desk and then looked up at Milly again. "As the time approaches, I can prescribe antibiotics and painkillers to make you more comfortable, but what we need is a miracle."

He sighed deeply and said, "The network has every available resource working on this issue, but they are not hopeful of positive results for years to come. Feeding on humans has become a game of Russian roulette for immortals, so I would rely on the serum as much as possible."

Milly looked him straight in the eye and asked, "Is Sasha at risk for being with me?"

"I cannot know for certain, but she does not display any of the symptoms, and if you don't share blood, there should be no reason to expect infection," Dr. Moore said.

Relieved by this news, Milly squeezed Sasha's hand tightly. "Thank you, Dr. Moore, for being honest with us," she said.

Sasha took Milly's lead and stood to leave the office. "Call or visit anytime you wish," he offered as he walked them to the door.

✝

Sasha closed the door of the car behind Milly and slowly walked around the side of the car. She located a hotel and booked a room for them to share the night. She got them checked in and when they settled into the room, she took Milly in her arms and held her close.

Milly burst into tears as she melted into Sasha's arms. Sasha moved them onto the bed and held Milly until she cried herself to sleep. Sasha watched Milly sleep fitfully as she thought back to Milly's past warning. Sasha had prepared for and survived the aging and death of her parents, but she never dreamed that Milly would become ill and die as well. Eternity together was rapidly approaching its end, coming all too fast for an ill-prepared Sasha. She snuggled into her lover's body and they slept the night away.

✝

The next morning as they snuggled in bed, Milly said, "I became infected the last night we fed in New Orleans. I have not felt well since then, so it must have been that man who infected me."

It was a moot point now, Sasha knew, but Milly took some comfort in uncovering the how and when that the infection occurred. "You will have to be even more careful now when you feed, my love," she said and then softly kissed Sasha.

"I will, I promise," Sasha said as she kissed Milly again.

They showered when they got out of bed and dressed for breakfast before heading back to Sugarland. Milly was unable to finish her meal and Sasha's appetite failed her as she watched her lover, still in a state of shock.

Milly sat close to Sasha as she drove, tucked underneath her arm as they journeyed south, her head resting on Sasha's shoulder. Sasha looked at her lover closely as she slept, and she imagined the turmoil Milly was feeling after receiving such dreaded news.

Milly woke as they turned into the long drive heading into Sugarland and looked up at Sasha with tears in her eyes. "I don't want to say anything to James and Martha yet," she said.

"I can understand that," Sasha said. "There is no hurry to share the news with anyone, so we will wait until you are ready."

Sasha parked the car and walked around to take Milly's arm as they walked into the house. James and Martha were in the kitchen and greeted them as they entered.

"Welcome home, ladies," Martha said. "I am cooking your favorite, Milly, chicken and dumplings." It was impossible for her to know the news they had received, but Sasha felt that Martha and James knew something wasn't right.

"They smell terrific," Milly said, managing a smile for Martha. "I want to lie down for a while, but I will be ready to eat by dinnertime."

"Would you like some homemade biscuits as well?" Martha asked. "James made a trip down to the honey tree today and brought in some fresh honey."

"That would be wonderful," Milly said, and allowed Sasha to lead her from the kitchen up to their bedroom. Sasha tucked her in under the covers and returned downstairs to retrieve their bag from the car.

James met her in the foyer carrying the bag, and the look he gave Sasha confirmed that both he and Martha knew something was drastically wrong.

"Thank you, James," Sasha said as she took the bag from him.

"You are welcome, Sasha," he said. "I will park the car and take care of the horses, but if there is anything you need, just let me know."

Sasha nodded her head as she placed the bag at the foot of the stairs and then walked into the kitchen for a glass of ice water. Martha saw her enter, walked over to Sasha, and hugged her close. Sasha was close to tears when Martha released her, and she realized it was impossible to hide anything from the couple that knew them so well.

"Just let us know how we can help," Martha said.

"Milly has not adjusted to the news we received yet. I promised to wait until she is ready to talk with you and James," Sasha said.

"We will be here for both of you whenever you need us to be," Martha said.

"Thank you, Martha, your kindness means a great deal to both of us," Sasha said as she went to the refrigerator and poured Milly a glass of ice water. Milly's thirst had increased since she first became sick and ice water was the only liquid that quenched the fire in her throat. "We will be down later for dinner."

"I could fix you both a tray and bring it upstairs," Martha suggested. "That way you both could relax."

"I will let you know what we decide," Sasha promised as she left the room with the ice water, stopping to pick up the bag before climbing the stairs to return to Milly.

†

Milly took the glass from Sasha, drank half its contents, and then settled back under the covers with a chill. "Will you hold me for a while?" Milly asked.

"Of course I will, my love," Sasha said with a smile.

Sasha removed her shoes, crept onto the bed beside her, and took Milly in her arms as her tears soaked Sasha's shoulder. Sasha attempted to fight off her own tears, trying to remain strong, but her heart was breaking for Milly as she sobbed against her body. Silent tears fled down Sasha's cheeks as she tried to comfort her lover.

†

She and Milly napped for nearly two hours before Sasha woke and asked if she was ready to eat. Milly nodded her head yes. "Do you feel up to going downstairs or would you prefer to eat here?"

"Let's go downstairs, my love. I am afraid we will be spending plenty of time in here in the months to come," Milly said.

Sasha knew Milly would be correct in her assumption and helped her out of the bed. They went downstairs and joined James and Martha in the kitchen. Martha smiled brightly when she saw Milly enter and went over to the stove to serve a large plate of chicken and dumplings for Milly while James placed a platter of hot biscuits on the table.

Sasha was relieved to see Milly eat a hearty meal. She hoped the food would help lift her spirits.

After dinner, Milly asked, "Will you play for me tonight?"

"I would love to, my dear," Sasha answered and took Milly to the love seat and covered her with a blanket before she started to play.

Milly listened to the music Sasha chose to play and her thoughts drifted back to the first time she heard Sasha play, so many years ago now, as a young student in London. She had fallen in love with her the moment she saw her seated at the baby grand at the Royal Albert, so young and full of excitement.

"What are you thinking, my love?" Sasha asked.

"I was thinking back to the day we met, when you snuck in to play the piano at the Royal Albert," Milly said.

"I most certainly did not sneak in. The door was left unlocked," Sasha said with a grin.

Sasha watched as Milly began to nod off and stopped playing to take her upstairs to bed. She tucked her under the blanket and found Milly's eyes watching her closely. "I was having the sweetest dream of our first kiss," she said as Sasha sat on the bed next to her.

Sasha leaned down to place her lips softly against Milly's and they shared a tender kiss. "Yes, it was like that one," Milly said after they ended the kiss. "After all these years they still taste just as sweet."

"There will be many more to come," Sasha promised as she slipped from her clothes and crawled into the bed beside Milly, wrapping her body around her lover. She caressed Milly's body until she quietly drifted off to sleep. Sasha's tears started again as she cried herself to sleep.

Chapter Twenty-five

Lost

The next few months stole away quickly and Sasha and Milly spent every waking moment together. Milly continued to go to the cottage to paint and Sasha would sit next to her and watch as she painted, more slowly, but just as beautifully as before. Sasha found Milly most beautiful while caught in the rapture of painting and one day had an idea while she sat watching Milly.

"You know what I find strange, my love?" Sasha said as they sprawled out across the bed after lunch.

"What, Sasha?" Milly said.

"Well, you painted the picture of me in London, which we gave to Theo, and that now hangs on the wall in the parlor, but there is no picture of you to complement it," Sasha said as her fingers stroked through Milly's hair. "Will you paint that picture now for me, my love?"

Milly looked deep into Sasha's eyes, tears threatening to fall. "Yes, Sasha, I will paint that picture for you," she said. "Please pick out a photograph of me that you like when we go back to the house tonight, and I will use that to paint a self-portrait."

"Deal." Sasha leaned down to kiss Milly's forehead. "You are running a fever," Sasha said as her lips touched her heated skin. "Would you like me to get you some ice water?"

"No, darling, please just hold me for a while," Milly said as she lay her head on Sasha's chest, smiling to herself when she heard the strong heartbeat deep in Sasha's chest. Even now in her debilitated state, their hearts continued to beat with the same rhythm. Her fingers softly stroked Sasha's face and traced the outline of the beautiful smile she loved so much.

Fate had been so cruel to them, Sasha thought as she held Milly. From the outside, Milly looked as healthy and vibrant as she always had, but inside her body was slowly losing the ability to protect and regenerate itself as the disease destroyed her organs.

When they returned to the house later that evening, Sasha and Milly turned the pages of the many photograph albums they had filled as the years passed. Sasha chose a photograph of Milly sitting astride her beloved Hera, her faithful horse long dead. Milly's smile was brilliant as she watched Sasha take the photograph. That smile more than anything else made Sasha choose that photograph, for Milly's smile made her heart melt, and though Milly was weak and felt horrible, she still managed to smile for the ones she loved.

✝

Weeks passed and Milly made slow progress on the self-portrait. The cane would be ready to harvest soon and Milly knew that James and Martha would be away for the two weeks necessary to burn the cane fields. Martha was allergic to the smoke, so she and James would take a trip to Baton Rouge to visit their children while the fields burned. Sasha and Milly would be alone during this time, precious moments to spend together as her time drew near, and Milly struggled to finish the portrait for Sasha.

✝

The evening before James and Martha were to leave for Baton Rouge, Milly asked them to join her in the parlor. Milly was propped on the love seat and covered with blankets as James and Martha pulled chairs close to her. Milly could see tears welling up in Martha's eyes as the woman looked at her.

"When you return from Baton Rouge, I will be gone," Milly said.

"Then we will not go," she said stubbornly.

"Yes, Martha, you will. Your allergies are horrible when the fields are burned, and I won't tolerate you staying behind for me," Milly said. "You and James have been our family for years, and I do not want you to mourn my passing as we will one day meet again. I need you to be strong for one another and for my beloved Sasha."

"Please Milly, let us be here for you," Martha implored.

"You have been there for me all these years, Martha and James, but this is a journey I must take on my own," Milly said bravely. "I have no words to express my appreciation for the love and kindness we have shared, so I will simply say thank you."

Martha broke down in tears and James placed his arm around his wife to comfort her. "Is there anything we can do for either of you, Milly?" James asked.

"Your family has always been good to us, James, and I hope that after you are gone, one of your children will return to care for Sasha, until the day comes when we meet again."

"Baby James has already said he wishes to return to Sugarland," James said, which surprised even Sasha.

"That gives me great comfort," Milly said. "Of all your beautiful children, Sugarland is in his blood and it makes me proud to know he will be returning to care for her."

"He plans to marry a fine young woman named Marie and then join us here to raise their children," Martha said.

Milly smiled. "It will be grand to have little ones running around Sugarland again."

"Yes, it will," she said. "It may also please you to know that James has said that his firstborn girl will be named after you. James said if it weren't for you tutoring him, he would have never made it to college and he loves you like a second mother."

Those words broke her resolve and Milly's tears began to flow. "I will miss you both so," she said when she finally regained her composure.

"You will still be right here with us," James said as he tapped his chest over his heart, his tears flowing freely now too.

Milly broke out in a coughing spell, and Martha returned to the kitchen for a glass of ice water. Milly was pale and weak when Martha returned with the drink and when her hand brushed Martha's as she took the glass, Martha could feel the chill in her skin.

Milly drank the cool liquid, and it temporarily soothed the fire in her body. She was ready to lie down and asked Sasha to take her upstairs.

"We will leave early in the morning, but there are casseroles and plenty of food in the freezer to hold you over until we return," Martha said. She and James kissed Milly's cheek as she stood and hugged them.

"Goodbye for now, my friends," Milly said, her eyes smiling with the love she had for them.

"We love you both," James said as he led Martha out of the parlor and to the front door. They stopped to watch Sasha and Milly as they slowly climbed the stairs.

"Goodbye, my friend," Martha whispered and followed James out the door.

James had barely closed the door when Martha's tears began in earnest and she collapsed into his arms. "What will we do now, James?" she asked through her tears.

"We will go to Baton Rouge to honor Milly's wishes and when we return we will be strong for Sasha. She will need our love and support more than ever," he said as he held his precious wife.

Once her tears were under control, she and James returned to their home to finalize preparations for their trip.

Chapter Twenty-six

Final Days

Sasha heard the motor of James and Martha's car as they drove away from Sugarland. She could also sense the tears that were flowing down Martha's cheeks as she sat beside James. Martha desperately wanted to be with Milly, but understood and accepted her decision to share her last days alone with Sasha.

Sasha woke early the next morning and rolled on to her side, watching Milly as she slept. They had been together for so many years that Sasha was lost while thinking of how she would survive without her. She was deep in memories they shared when Milly's hand reached over to stroke her face.

"Good morning, my love," she whispered.

"Good morning, I hope I didn't wake you," Sasha said, lowering her face to brush Milly's lips with hers.

"You didn't," Milly said. "My body says it is time to wake and get moving. I think I would like to start with a nice bath today."

"Then a nice bath is what you will have, my dear," Sasha said as she climbed from the bed to start the bathwater.

Sasha helped Milly from the bed and led her into the bathroom. She raised the nightgown above Milly's head and did not speak of the blood spots that dotted the front of the gown. There was no need in upsetting Milly further. She helped Milly into the tub and then soaped a large sponge and began to bathe her lover. She carefully shampooed Milly's hair that had now grown past her shoulders and Sasha took her time as she enjoyed running her fingers through the thick curls.

Milly soaked for a few minutes after Sasha completed her bath and allowed the tepid water to soothe muscles that ached from the coughing spells that painfully ripped through her chest. As she laid her head back against the bath pillow, Sasha asked, "What do you think you can eat this morning?"

"I would love a large glass of cold milk and some toast with honey and peanut butter mixed together," Milly said with a smile.

"That's an easy breakfast to prepare," Sasha said as she stood to retrieve a large bath sheet to wrap Milly in. "Ready when you are."

Milly carefully stood and stepped from the bathtub. Sasha wrapped the towel around her body and patted her dry. She towel-dried her hair and then picked up a brush to gently brush her hair free of tangles. They brushed their teeth and then headed down to the kitchen.

Milly sat at the table and watched as Sasha prepared her breakfast, pouring milk over a glass of ice to get it cold. She carried the milk to the table then mixed the honey and peanut butter and spread it across the toasted bread. "I am going to scramble some eggs, are you sure you wouldn't like some?" she asked.

"Not this morning, my love, but thanks," Milly said as she took a bite of her toast.

Sasha cooked the eggs, and then sat at the table with Milly. "What would you like to do today?" she asked.

"I want to work on the portrait as long as I can today," Milly said.

"Would you like me to bring your supplies up to the house?" Sasha asked.

"No, I would like you to drive me down to the cottage. It has been so long, I wouldn't know how to paint elsewhere," she teased.

Sasha knew how important it was for Milly to finish the portrait, but she also dreaded the day it was complete, as she feared that would be the last day of Milly's life. Milly would depart this world granting Sasha's final request. Sasha had to fight back the tears that threatened to overcome her.

Milly ate three of the slices of toast and drank two glasses of milk before she and Sasha went upstairs to dress. Milly chose a loose pair of pants and one of Sasha's T-shirts to wear, and watched as Sasha slipped on a pair of jeans and a T-shirt. With a smile, Sasha stood before her love and offered her arm for assistance. Milly gratefully looped her hands around Sasha's arm and they walked from the house. Milly sat on the porch steps while Sasha went for the car. The birds were singing happily that morning and the sun was bright and warm. Later that day Milly knew the skies would be black with smoke from cane fields burning, so she soaked in the blue sky and fluffy white clouds.

Sasha pulled the car around and assisted Milly into the passenger's seat. She closed the door behind her and walked around to climb behind the wheel. Sasha drove slowly down the path to the cottage, careful not to jostle Milly's body and cause her unnecessary pain. She pulled the car close to the front door, offered her arm again to Milly, and escorted her into the cottage to sit before her easel. Sasha stretched out on a small love seat across the room from her as she watched her lover prepare to paint.

Milly took great pride in mixing the oils to gain the precise colors she wanted to use and once she had finished, she began stroking the canvas with loving caresses as the painting came to life before her eyes. She remembered the day Sasha took the photograph. She and Sasha had saddled up the horses and ridden out to one of their favorite spots at the artesian well for a picnic.

The day had been glorious and they spread their blanket, made love underneath the ancient oak, and later dined on cold cuts, cheese, and a bottle of wine. Milly remembered lying in Sasha's arms as they watched the big fluffy clouds float by and they pointed out shapes and objects in them. She and Sasha had shared so much during their time together, and there was so much to be thankful. She had a lover that adored her, who had been faithful over the many years of their life together. Sasha had been her mate for over sixty years and each day felt as fresh and new as the first they shared together.

Sasha watched as Milly painted with deep concentration and wondered where her thoughts had drifted.

"A penny for your thoughts, pretty lady," she said as she adjusted a pillow under her head.

Milly stopped painting to turn toward Sasha. "I was thinking back to the day this photograph was taken."

Sasha smiled back at her. "I remember making love with you and then spending the remainder of the afternoon wrapped in our blanket as we watched the clouds float by."

"Maybe we could go there this week," Milly said and then remembered the fields would be burning. "Well, maybe after they finish the fields, we can go."

Sasha prayed that Milly would still be with her when the burning finished and would take her anywhere she wanted to go. "I hope they will finish quickly this year," Sasha said as Milly turned back to the canvas.

"Hopefully," Milly said as she began to caress the canvas again with her brush. She painted for two hours that day and when she stopped, she felt a few more days would be enough to complete the portrait. Her hands were trembling when she put away her supplies and turned back toward Sasha.

"Will you take me home for a nap, my darling?" Milly asked.

"I will take you anywhere you wish to go," Sasha said as she stood and walked over to her side.

They returned to the house and Sasha picked Milly up in her arms and carried her up the stairs to prevent Milly from exhausting the remainder of her strength. She placed her gently on the bed and removed her shoes before pulling the covers over her body. "Are you hungry or thirsty, my love?" Sasha asked.

"Some ice water would be nice, but I am not hungry at the moment," Milly said as she smiled weakly.

Sasha knew she was in pain and would offer her a pain pill when she returned with the water. She kissed Milly's fevered forehead, walked down to the kitchen, and returned with a pitcher of ice water and a glass. She filled a glass and helped Milly prop up on her pillows to allow her to drink. "Would you like a pain pill?" she asked.

"No, I want to spend the day with you and not sleeping," she said as she took the water.

"I will be right here beside you, Milly, so why don't you take the edge off your pain," she suggested.

Milly relented and took one of the small tablets from Sasha, chasing it down with a long drink of cold water.

Sasha sat the glass back on the bedside table then moved around to the opposite side of the bed. She removed her clothing and crept carefully under the covers as Milly settled back onto her pillows. Sasha snuggled into Milly's heated body and began to caress her lover's skin with her soft hands. Her hand slid beneath the baggy T-shirt and stroked across her stomach as Milly's hands played in Sasha's hair. Her hand moved further up Milly's body, gently brushing her erect nipples and Milly moaned loudly.

Milly pulled Sasha's face up for a tender kiss as Sasha's fingers continued to brush across her nipples.

Sasha used her hand to raise the shirt above Milly's breasts, moved her mouth down to cover a nipple with her soft mouth, and rolled her tongue over the excited nipple.

"Oh yes, Sasha," Milly said as she took Sasha's hand and moved it further down her body.

Sasha's hand slipped beneath the waistband of Milly's pants and her fingers caressed the dampness hidden between her thighs. Milly arched her back, filling Sasha's mouth with the soft flesh of her breast and spread her thighs, inviting her lover to enter her. Sasha suckled the breast as her fingers parted the swollen lips and disappeared into Milly's body.

Milly groaned her pleasure and her hips began to rock onto Sasha's fingers as she brought Milly to her peak, moving faster and deeper inside her. Milly's inner muscles convulsed around Sasha's fingers as her body released her pleasure, and Sasha withdrew and laid her head on Milly's shoulder. She watched a contented smile play across her lover's face as she closed her eyes and fell into a deep sleep.

Chapter Twenty-seven

The Last Kiss

The next day the rains came. The skies opened to drench the earth, extinguishing the fires in the field. Milly and Sasha stayed in bed all day, listening to the pounding of the rain on the tin roof and laughing over photographs in the albums as they flipped through page after page of their lives together. She was initially saddened by the rain as she would not be able to paint, but the time spent together was a treasure for them, and they collapsed on the bed, their sides aching from the laughter.

Later that evening, as the rains tapered off, Milly and Sasha walked out onto the front porch. When they looked up, a clear night sky and millions of stars were twinkling back at them, greeting them. Sasha returned inside, came back with a towel, and dried the porch swing. She and Milly sat on the swing and watched the beauty of a meteor storm as shooting stars fell to the earth. Hours later when the show was over, Sasha looked down and found Milly asleep on her shoulder.

She carefully bundled her lover in her arms, carried her up the stairs, and laid her gently on the bed. The moonlight streamed through the window and coated Milly with its light and Sasha fell in love with the beautiful woman all over again. A cloud passed in front of the moon, cloaking Milly in darkness and Sasha remembered that soon she would be gone from this life. She cried the tears she had held back all day. She cried tears for Milly, and for herself.

211

Nothing could prepare her for their eternity together to be over. She silently cursed the night Milly became infected.

Sasha dried her tears and climbed into bed next to Milly, her naked body pressed close to her lover to bathe in the warmth of her body. Sasha listened to the beating of Milly's heart and allowed its soothing sound to entice her to sleep.

†

The next morning dawned beautifully and Milly felt strong and eager to resume her painting. Sasha took her to the cottage and watched as she painted for three hours before tiring. The painting was nearly complete; another morning should have the last strokes done. Then they would let the paint dry thoroughly before they framed it and hung it in the parlor. As she looked at the portrait, Sasha could almost feel the warmth from the smile Milly was wearing, and was amazed by how lifelike the painting had become.

Sasha carried Milly upstairs for her afternoon nap. Once settled on the bed, Milly asked, "Sasha, in the closet there is a small box, would you bring it to me?"

Sasha found the box Milly was requesting and handed the package to Milly with a quizzical look on her face.

"Sit with me please and open the box for me," Milly said.

Sasha sat next to her and carefully opened the package. She peeled back the wrapping material to reveal a bronze urn. The tears returned to Sasha's eyes as she reached in and took the urn from its package.

"When I am gone, I want you to place my ashes in this urn," Milly said. "I know it is pointless to ask you not to mourn for me, so I will make only one request." Milly took the urn in her hands. "Keep my ashes for only one year anywhere you wish, but on the first anniversary of my death, I want you to set me free." Sasha looked at Milly with tears streaming down her cheeks. "I want you to spread my ashes around our little cottage, at the main house, and then the rest I would like you to leave at our little clearing by the artesian well."

Sasha nodded her head to agree to Milly's request as the ability to speak was beyond her reach.

"Those are the places where I have shared the most cherished moments with you, and I wish to remain a part of Sugarland forever."

"I am not ready to let you go," Sasha managed as she cradled the urn in her hands.

"I have another day or two," Milly said, "but the time is growing near." Milly's hands caressed Sasha's cheek and wiped the tears from her face. "We have been fortunate enough to share many years, and I will always be with you in your heart and in your memories. I am thankful for that." She brought Sasha's face down to hers and softly kissed her lips. "I am blessed to have had you for my mate, and I hope after I am gone, you will find someone else who makes you as happy as you have made me."

"There will never be another you," Sasha said.

"No, there won't," Milly said. "But, there will be another who comes into your life one day that will make you happy again When she arrives I want you to embrace her and take her for your own."

Sasha was unprepared for this conversation and could not fathom the true meaning of Milly's words. Milly was foretelling her future, but all she wanted to feel was the present and not waste a moment of their precious time together. Milly took the urn from Sasha's hands and placed it on the bedside table.

"Come hold me," she said to Sasha.

Sasha stretched across the bed, took Milly in her arms, and held her close for the remainder of the day. That evening she baked them a casserole and then she played for Milly until her head began to nod. She carried Milly up to bed where they lay side-by-side, looking at one another, and gently touching until Milly's eyes could no longer remain open. Sasha watched over her for hours as she slept, and in the small hours of the morning, snuggled into Milly's warmth and slept as well.

†

Milly finished the painting the following morning and Sasha placed the easel in front of the window for the sun to dry her canvas. Milly was proud of the portrait and happy she had the strength left to finish before she passed on. She and Sasha spent the remainder of the afternoon snuggled on the small bed, looking at the portrait and talking quietly.

Milly's appetite had returned that evening, and Sasha cooked her favorite meal of chicken and dumplings with hot biscuits and fresh green beans. Milly ate a hearty meal and fell asleep in Sasha's arms a short while later.

†

The next morning, Milly announced she wanted to ride into New Orleans. Sasha placed her gently into the car and drove carefully into the city. They rode past their first home, the café that was still a thriving business and then down along the river. They parked the car and walked along the levee for a while before returning for the trip home. For a few hours, it was if there were nothing wrong with Milly, her steps strong and sure, but as the day wore on her strength waned with the setting sun.

214

After a light dinner and a soaking bath, they relaxed on the bed. Milly was snuggled in Sasha's strong arms when she looked up at Sasha. "Make love with me one last time," she said.

Tears glistened in Sasha's eyes as she slowly removed the nightgown from Milly's thin body and slipped out of her clothing. She lay down next to her lover and began to caress her skin, each stroke of her fingers memorizing the texture and contours of her lover's body, as this would truly be the last opportunity they would have to share their physical love.

Sasha kissed Milly's lips softly as her hands caressed her body. Their sensual kisses turned hungry as the fire burned between them. Sasha parted her lips with her tongue and explored Milly's mouth, their tongues entwining in a slow rhythmic dance. Her hands cupped and kneaded the soft mounds of Milly's breasts and her thumbs glided over erect nipples as her moans grew louder. She kissed her way down from Milly's lips to her ear and softly whispered, "I will always love you," into Milly's ear. The warm breath and enduring devotion of her words sent a shiver of delight through Milly's body.

Sasha's tongue softly licked at the sensitive skin of Milly's neck, and she traced the jugular down to the base of her neck before she moved to Milly's breast. The tip of her tongue swirled slowly around Milly's nipples, raising gooseflesh across her body as her hands stroked down her sides. Sasha gently lowered her body onto Milly's as she took a soft breast into her mouth. She could feel Milly's wetness grow across her stomach as she suckled each breast gently before the rushing of Milly's breathing urged her on.

Sasha moved down between Milly's thighs and her head dipped lower, her outstretched tongue seeking the well of her lover's wetness. Her fingers tenderly parted the swollen lips that protected the sweet nectar and with the tip of her tongue, Sasha gently probed as the sweetness began to flow. She drank deeply of Milly's wetness, licking slowly and entering her deeply with her tongue until Milly's body shook with pleasure, and she cried out, "Oh yes, Sasha."

Sasha moved back up her body and they shared a deep hungry kiss as Milly's fingers slid deep inside Sasha's body. Sasha rocked her hips against her fingers, driving Milly deeper inside with each stroke, until Sasha was panting for air. Her mouth was next to Milly's ear as her hand slid down between Milly's trembling thighs and entered her. "Come with me, my love," Sasha said as her fingers drove into Milly in rhythm with the movement of their bodies. Soon they were both shuddering in climax, their bodies glowing with a fine layer of perspiration.

Sasha smiled and the sparkle in Milly's eyes made her body go weak. She held her close until Milly fell asleep and was still embracing her when Milly's labored breathing woke her the next morning.

Sasha was alarmed and about to panic until Milly opened her eyes and the peace she found in them put her at rest. "Is there anything I can get you?" she asked.

"One last kiss," Milly said as she smiled at Sasha.

Sasha leaned down and pressed her lips against Milly's for a tender, lingering kiss. When she raised her head again she glimpsed the waning sparkle in Milly's eyes, and with a deep sigh of contentment, Milly was gone.

I have loved you for forever, Milly projected as her spirit slipped away.

Sasha burst into tears as she cradled Milly's lifeless body in her arms and rocked back and forth on the bed. Sasha felt the chill that had taken Milly's life fade as her body filled with a growing heat. Sasha held her until forced to lay her body back onto the bed.

"Oh no, Milly, don't leave me yet," Sasha cried.

She watched in horror as Milly's milky white skin darkened to a deep brown and then her body started smoldering. Sasha sat in shock as an inner fire consumed the woman she loved, and her body reduced to a small pile of ash.

Sasha cried for nearly an hour before she could regain control of her body and climbed from the bed to open the urn that would hold Milly's ashes. She carefully scooped the ashes and let them run over the palm of her hand into the urn. Like the sands of an hourglass, Milly's life flowed smoothly into the urn where she would rest for a year as she had requested. Sasha then carefully returned the lid to seal the urn and held it gently in her hands.

She walked down the stairs and placed the urn on the mantel next to where Milly's portrait would hang. She then walked out onto the porch as the sun began to rise and let out a howl of pain that was so fierce it silenced the creatures in the bayou. Sasha fell to her knees and wept for the loss of her love as the sky opened and the rain began to fall.

Chapter Twenty-eight

Alone

Sasha did not eat or sleep for the next three days. She tried without success to numb her broken heart with alcohol, but succeeded only in fueling her rage. On the fourth day she sat in the small stone cottage Milly loved so dearly, looking at the final portrait Milly had painted. She stared at the painting until her exhaustion overwhelmed her and her body collapsed onto the small bed. She buried her face in the pillow searching for Milly's scent and slept until the next afternoon. "I love you, Milly," she whispered through her tears.

The rest of the week Sasha tried to keep her mind occupied and spent her days riding Titan across the property and watching as the workers finished burning the fields. At night, she roamed the bayou, hunting. On her third night, she discovered a lone poacher and took her rage out on his body, draining him dry and feeding his body to a pair of hungry alligators, who were probably the prey he was hunting. What irony, she thought. The man was out to poach and the very creatures he sought to slaughter for his benefit made a nice dinner of him.

As the skies cleared and the thick black smoke disappeared for another year, Sasha prepared for the return of James and Martha. She washed the dishes that had accumulated in the sink and bathed her tired body. Sasha hoped a good night's sleep would remove the dark circles that had formed under her eyes. After eating a light dinner,

Sasha took the portrait of Milly and framed it before hanging it on the wall next to her own. She then sat on the love seat and stared at the portrait. As her eyes searched the portrait, something caught her attention and she walked over to look more closely at the painting. Sasha could not believe what her eyes were seeing. Deep in the leaves of the trees in the portrait, Milly had shaped the clusters of leaves to form a message.

Sasha laughed loudly as her eyes traced the letters of her message, which read, "Sasha, I love you." Even in the grip of death, Milly had left a message that only Sasha would know to look for. Sasha said, "I love you too, Milly Vansant," to an empty house.

The following day James and Martha returned to Sugarland. Though Sasha had taken great comfort from Milly's message, the dark circles remained beneath her eyes. Martha took one look at how thin Sasha had become and immediately stormed to the kitchen to start cooking. James and Sasha walked out to the stable to feed the horses while she cooked.

"How are you holding up?" James asked.

"The first few days were pure hell, but Milly's love will give me the strength to make it through," Sasha said.

"We know how much you loved one another, so if there is anything we can do to make the hard times easier for you, please come to us," James said.

"Just having the both of you here is a great comfort to me, James," Sasha said. "I honestly don't know what I would do here alone."

"You are a strong woman, Sasha, and though you might not feel it now, you will come through this period even stronger," he said. James placed a fatherly hand on her shoulder. "The love the two of you shared is rare, and will be enough to carry you through this lifetime."

They finished tending the horses and walked back to the house together just as Martha was serving bowls of gumbo. She carried a platter of steaming corn bread and a pitcher of tea to the table and then gave Sasha a hearty hug. "Now you will eat, young lady, and put some meat back on those bones of yours," she said.

"It is good to have you back, Martha," Sasha said with a small smile as she returned her hug.

After the meal, Sasha led them into the parlor and showed them the portrait Milly had finished and they marveled at how lifelike it was. She also showed them the bronze urn sitting on the mantel, telling them of Milly's wish to have her ashes spread a year after her death. Though they thought it was odd that Sasha did not give Milly a proper funeral, they understood the uniqueness of Milly's request and knew Sasha would make her wish a reality.

"We are here for you always, Sasha," James said. "Please do not hesitate to call on us any hour of the day if you need anything."

"Just having the two of you here is a great comfort to me," Sasha said. "I don't know how I could survive without you."

James and Martha hugged Sasha and returned to their home, leaving her in the parlor gazing at the portrait.

Life slowly returned to normal at Sugarland and business prospered. They had postponed future reservations for the bed-and-breakfast while Milly was ill, but once they returned from Baton Rouge, Sasha announced it was time to resume business.

James and Martha tended to the bed-and-breakfast guests and Sasha worked the books and managed the reservations. Sasha spent very little time with their guests, preferring to depend on James and Martha to run the business while she sank deeper in her mourning.

When the fall returned and James and Martha took their annual trip, Sasha was alone again to grant Milly's final wish.

"Are you sure you don't want us to stay with you this year?" Martha said.

"No, Martha, this I have to do alone. You and James need to go on your holiday as planned."

As she promised, exactly one year from the date of her death, Sasha took the urn down from the mantel and carried it outside. She removed the lid and sprinkled some of Milly's ashes across the front lawn. A light breeze carried Milly's ashes across the lawn making them disappear. Sasha walked to the barn and saddled Titan. She picked up the urn, mounted the gallant steed, and rode to the cottage.

"I will always remember the time we spent here," Sasha spoke softly.

Since Milly's death, Sasha had visited less and less frequently as the memory of Milly was so strong inside the stone walls of the cottage, but she still had Martha clean the place weekly. Sasha scattered some of the ashes around the front window, then she stepped inside the cottage. Milly's easel and brushes still sat in front of the window where for so many hours she sat painting. Sasha picked up one of Milly's brushes as she sat in her chair for a moment and gazed out of the window.

"I can remember the last days when you fought the sickness so hard to finish the portrait for me," Sasha said with tears in her eyes. "I never told you, but that was your most beautiful painting and I will cherish it forever."

Titan whinnied quietly to bring Sasha back to reality, and she took the urn and mounted the horse again. They rode to the special clearing which held the artesian well. Sasha opened the valve and fresh water filled the small trough where Titan drank freely. Sasha took the tin cup and dipped a cold drink for herself. She then opened the urn, scattered the remainder of Milly's ashes around the clearing, and then sat beneath the ancient oak.

"You always loved this spot," Sasha said as she watched the last of Milly's ashes floating in the breeze.

Instead of the tears she expected, Sasha smiled as she thought back to the time she and Milly had spent under the tree. She laid her head back against the worn bark. "Welcome home, my love," Sasha said.

Sasha dozed off with her memories of Milly. Titan nuzzling into her neck woke her hours later.

"I know Titan, it's time to go home," she said as she hugged the large horse's neck.

A light breeze had come up and Sasha imagined she could hear Milly whisper her name as the breeze blew through the leaves. She smiled and looked down at her watch to find that four hours had passed since she left the house. Though she still missed Milly horribly, Sasha felt rejuvenated that she had fulfilled her lover's last request. As she placed her foot in the stirrup and pulled herself into the saddle, Sasha felt a burden lift from her spirit.

Sasha understood then what Milly had meant when she told her to mourn for her for only one year and that the scattering of her ashes would be the beginning of a new chapter of Sasha's life.

When James and Martha returned, they noticed the peacefulness in Sasha immediately and they knew her period of mourning was over. Martha cooked a batch of chicken and dumplings and together they celebrated Milly's passing.

"It is so good to see you smiling again," Martha said.

"I will always love her, but now that I have fulfilled her last request, I feel Milly is at home." Sasha smiled. "Now Milly will be a part of Sugarland forever."

†

Later that year, Sasha welcomed James Jr. and his young wife, Marie, back to Sugarland. James Sr. suffered a massive heart attack during the next spring in the garden and he died toiling among his precious vegetables. Martha was heartbroken by her loss and mourned herself into her grave nearly six months later.

As the years wore on, Sasha remained faithful to the memory of Milly's love, content to survive on the memories they had shared. Many times Sasha thought back to her last days with Milly and the conversation they had about someone new coming into Sasha's life, but she continued to discard the idea that anyone could ever replace her beloved.

"I will love you for an eternity," Sasha said as she stared at the portrait and the woman smiling back at her.

The End.

Bayou Justice

Sequel to Sugarland

Sneek Peek

Chapter One

Sasha crept out of her comfortable bed to pull the drapes in the master bedroom that were preventing the early morning sunlight from streaming in. Sasha spent the previous night tossing and turning as she relived the past thirty years of her life without Milly. She wearily crawled back into her bed for a few more hours of slumber before she would have to rise in preparation for her arriving guests.

✝

For the past eighty-five years, Sasha Thibodaux had owned Sugarland Plantation, a working sugar cane farm that she leased out to local farmers. Besides this income, the history of Sugarland as a haunted plantation had added to her wealth. The bed and breakfast business had prospered and there was a long waiting list for reservations, many of whom were returning patrons year after year. Sasha seldom traveled far from Sugarland and when she did, she felt her heart longing for the comfort and seclusion of her home.

Sasha spent time after Milly's death learning more about the specters that lingered at Sugarland. Lizette was a seven-year-old child who had succumbed to the same flu pandemic in 1919 that had taken Sasha's mother. Visitors frequently reported sightings of her skipping through the halls or playing the baby grand in the plantation's ample parlor. Several times as Sasha played the piano, she sensed Lizette's presence in the room and would at times catch a glimpse of the child dancing through the room to the music she was playing.

Luscious was a slave who had gone into the bayou to retrieve catfish from a trotline for the master's dinner. When he reached into the water, an alligator attacked him, severing his left arm from his body. Luscious was able to make his way back to the plantation, but died several days later from the loss of blood and infection. Over the years, and especially during the full moon, visitors have spotted Luscious walking down the path toward the bayou, or roaming through the cane fields.

Finally yet importantly, is Joshua. Joshua, a beautiful young slave, hanged from the old oak out front when the landowner caught him in a compromising position with his daughter. Joshua was only sixteen when he died for his indiscretion. Visitors have seen Joshua, sitting under the oak where he hanged, weeping for his lost love. Of all the ghosts, Sasha felt closest to Joshua, as she understood the pain from the loss of a loved one.

Sasha felt at home with these specters, however, at times she longed for companionship. She detested the fact that she had to still feed on humans from time to time to continue her existence, and the loss of Milly, kept her secluded from the outside world. Sasha doubted she could survive losing another lover, preferring instead to dream of Milly and the love they had shared.

†

The Network, a specialized laboratory in Atlanta, was working to create a liquid serum to replace the need for vampires to feed on humans to maintain their existence, while living in harmony with the prey they had feasted on for a thousand years. The progress on perfecting the serum was painfully slow. Sasha and Milly had started with the serum years before, but the effect was not enough to prevent the need for feeding completely. Maybe if the serum been further developed at the time, it would have prevented Milly from being infected. Instead, she suffered the horrible disease that took her from Sasha. Their efforts were gallant, but the hunger burned deep within her and the synthetic blood the Network had developed could not satisfy the lust for human blood that made her nights unbearably restless. Sasha would battle the hunger until she could no longer tolerate the pain. She would then surrender and set out to hunt the bayou, to feast on a lone poacher, knowing the carnivorous denizens of the swamp were more than willing to dispose of the corpse to prevent detection.

†

Sasha lay in bed contemplating a night of hunting when Marie came to the door gently tapping. "Sasha, you awake?" she quietly asked her.

"Yes, Marie, what is it?" Sasha replied.

Marie and her husband James, while not blessed with Sasha's immortality, rewarded with an excessively slow aging process and had served her well for many years. They were the second generation to reside at Sugarland and Sasha was thankful for their years of service. Marie slowly entered the room and found Sasha lying on the bed.

"I wanted to let you know that James was going to drive me to town to purchase supplies before he leaves for the airport to pick up the guests. Is there anything I can get you before we leave?"

"No thank you, Marie," Sasha said. "I am going to laze around a while this morning and then I will prepare for our guests as well," she continued.

"Very well then Sasha, we will be back shortly," Marie said as she left the room and closed the door.

Sasha lie back on her bed and mentally reviewed the guest list. Four sorority sisters from Tulane were meeting at Sugarland for a long weekend reunion. The four women had not visited one another for several years and were excited about catching up with their old friends. Lisa Thomas had been in regular contact with her as the organizer of the trip.

Lisa, a schoolteacher from Jackson, had arranged to sample some of the nightlife in nearby New Orleans while sharing the secluded resort with her college mates. She was successful in persuading Kara Stewart, a criminal attorney from Atlanta, to leave the rush of her busy practice behind and Susan Schultz, a successful realtor in Asheville, was looking forward to the slower pace of the bayou. Cindy Search, the lone married woman of the four, welcomed the change from the doldrums associated with life as the wife of a prominent banker in Charleston.

Their host had made plans for the women to have a private ghost tour in New Orleans on Friday after a day of shopping at The River Walk. Marie would be busy cooking her fabulous creations while James would provide transportation for the women during the weekend. Sasha would join her guests for drinks before the evening meal, but for the most part Marie and James would attend to their needs.

†

Unable to sleep, Sasha decided to shower and dress for a ride around the property. As she dressed, she smiled at the misconception that modern vampires could not cast an appearance in a mirror. She gazed into the mirror, her deep lavender eyes framed by shoulder-length black hair, which, surprisingly, was lacking gray hairs for a person of one hundred and fifteen. Pleased with the reflection smiling back at her, she stepped out into a bright sunny day.

†

She walked to the stables and saddled up Thunder, her favorite mount. Sugarland encompassed over five hundred acres and she took pleasure in riding over the property. Sasha eased Thunder into a gentle trot and rode past one of the sugar cane fields in the process of harvesting. Sasha waved to the foreman, who was barking out orders to the migrant workers harvesting the crop. The man cautiously raised his hand to wave back as the hairs on the back of his neck snapped to attention. A shiver passed through his body as her eyes fixed him with a cloaked stare. The foreman was relieved when she and Thunder were no longer in sight and again began shouting at the workers cutting the cane.

The harvesting of the cane had always been a painful time for Sasha since Milly's death. In the next few weeks, the harvest would be complete and she would celebrate another anniversary of her lover's death. "I still love you so," Sasha, said her voice filled with sadness.

†

Sasha and Thunder cantered around the property. They were returning to the stable, when she saw James arriving with the carload of guests. Leading Thunder to the stables to allow him to cool, she watched as James ushered the women into the house and then returned to unload their luggage. She walked up to the house as James removed the last of the bags from the trunk of the car. Taking one from the man, she walked with him into the house. Marie greeted the guests and seated the women in the parlor. She served them cool drinks while they waited to settle in their rooms.

"I think you are really going to enjoy this group of guests, Sasha," James said with a devilish grin. He was surprised at how eerily one of the young women resembled Milly.

"Oh really, James, why is that?" Sasha asked.

"You will see for yourself shortly," James said, barely able to contain a soft laugh.

Sasha looked at him quizzically, but followed him into the house curious to get an answer to her question.

She set the bag she was carrying on the floor in the foyer and stepped into the parlor. Removing her sunglasses as she walked in, she said, "Good afternoon and welcome to Sugarland. My name is Sasha and my staff, James, Marie and I, will do everything possible to meet your needs this weekend," she added with a brilliant smile. Sasha noted that one of the women was intently studying the painting of Milly. When the woman turned around, Sasha understood why she was so interested in the portrait. Sasha felt her knees go weak when she looked at the woman, whose likeness to Milly was uncanny. The young woman could easily pass for a descendant of Milly's.

The women introduced themselves, which allowed Sasha a moment to regain her composure, and then she moved forward to shake hands with Kara, the woman who had been studying the portrait. She fixed her lavender eyes on her, and heard the beating of Kara's heart jump noticeably. A slight blush graced Kara's face as Sasha held her hand for a moment longer than necessary as Sasha's eyes took in the beauty of the woman standing before her. Kara's sparkling blue eyes, framed by her light-brown hair, which fell to her shoulders reminded her so of Milly. Sasha's eyes drifted lower, marveling at the petite features of Kara's body. Sasha could feel the blood racing through Kara's veins as she smiled and continued to greet her guests.

"Marie will have fresh crawfish and cocktails prepared at five if you would like to settle into your rooms and freshen up from your travels. Dinner will be served at six and then you can make yourself at home and relax for the evening," she added.

"That sounds like a great plan," Lisa said as she rose from her seat.

Sasha watched as Marie escorted the four women down the hall and took an opportunity to dip into Kara's thoughts.

'I will definitely be visiting you later,' Sasha projected.

Kara turned to look back at Sasha grinning broadly and then rushed to catch her friends. Sasha enjoyed sending her mischievous thoughts into unsuspecting victims and watching as they responded to her suggestions. The young woman had stirred something deep in Sasha and for the first time in ages, Sasha felt her heart racing at the sight of her guest.

Sasha walked into her room and quickly stripped off her riding clothes and boots before starting the shower. She slipped under the tepid water and slowly caressed her body with the fragrant soap, eliminating the evidence of her afternoon ride in the humid bayou. Her fingers softly brushed across her hardened nipples as she closed her eyes and imagined Kara's hands roaming her needy body. It had been much too long since Sasha had had the pleasure of a lover, and she looked forward to seducing the young, alluring lawyer.

Kara's physical features reminded Sasha so much of Milly and her heart sank with melancholy memories of the great love she had lost nearly thirty years ago. Sasha's heart still ached for the love that she thought would last for eternity. Sasha remembered the conversation she and Milly had about a woman in her future that would return the love and passion Sasha had to offer which left her curious to know whether Kara could be the one Milly had seen in her future.

Sasha shook off the melancholy feeling and after dressing; she sprayed rich smelling cologne along her neckline and across her wrists, and walked to the parlor to join her guests for cocktails. She sat comfortably in an oversized chair across from Kara where she could easily capture her gaze with quietly seductive glances.

†

Marie poured a glass of red wine and handed it to Sasha before disappearing into the kitchen to finish preparing the crawfish.

"Sugarland is approximately three hundred years old and, as you can imagine, it was a plantation served by slaves. The owner, however, was a gentle slave master and treated his servants with a gentility not normally seen in most southern plantations. It wasn't until after his death that the first violence occurred at Sugarland, when his son found his daughter in a rather intimate situation with a young slave named Joshua," Sasha began as her guests sat listening intently to her history lesson. "Her father was so enraged that he had the young man hanged and shipped his daughter off to finishing school," Sasha continued. "The landowner, just as many of his era, felt it was entirely proper for him to take pleasure from the many female slaves, but he would not tolerate this behavior from his daughter."

Marie returned and served the crawfish cocktails as Sasha paused in her story.

"After the emancipation, the plantation was passed down from father to son for several generations until I purchased the property, and here we are today," Sasha continued to explain. "Sugar cane is still the primary crop and the lease for the land is very lucrative, allowing me the opportunity to use the house as an exclusive resort. I am sure Lisa has shared with you that Sugarland has a reputation for being haunted." Motioning toward Lisa, she said, "Keep your eyes and ears open during your stay." Sasha pointed upward and continued, "The full moon occurs tomorrow night which will be a prime time for a possible haunting."

Lisa asked several questions regarding the three known ghosts of Sugarland and Sasha answered them professionally while glancing at Kara several times to gauge her response to the sordid history. Sasha smiled when she noted the pulse jumping along Kara's neck, the beating of her heart pounding in Sasha's ears.

Marie entered the room, announced that dinner was ready, and led the four women into the dining room. Sasha excused herself from her guests and walked down to the stables to care for Thunder and the other horses housed there. After feeding them, she took a soft brush into Thunder's stall and brushed the magnificent stallion down after their long ride. His ears pricked forward, listening as she lovingly stroked his forehead.

"We will go out again soon," she promised as she slipped an extra-large block of hay in the bin and closed the door to his stall. She knew James would have devotedly tended to the horses, but she enjoyed the task of taking care of her powerful creatures.

†

Sasha sat on the porch in a well-worn rocking chair and watched as the sun slipped below the horizon and the night creatures came to life. Fireflies danced across the front yard to the music created by the crickets. Deep in the bayou, Sasha could hear the bellow of a bull alligator as he sought a mate. The concert of the night was interrupted by the slight creak of the door as it opened and Sasha intuitively knew that Kara was about to join her on the porch.

"Mind if I join you?" Kara asked politely.

"Of course not," Sasha said as she motioned her toward a rocking chair.

Kara reached into her pocket and lit a cigarette, offering one to Sasha.

"Thanks," Sasha said as she took the offered gift and breathed deeply of the cool menthol.

"I had forgotten how peaceful it can be in the bayou," Kara spoke as she slowly rocked back and forth. "Much different from Atlanta," she added with a quick smile.

"I hope you will take full advantage of your time here to relax and take every pleasure Sugarland has to offer," Sasha said as she locked eyes with Kara.

"I would very much like that," Kara replied, not sure if it was a sexual innuendo that she read into her host's statement. "I noticed you riding a fabulous stallion as we drove up," she said. "Is there any chance of getting a horseback tour while I am here?"

"I am sure that can be arranged," Sasha responded. "I do believe Lisa has plans for a river boat cruise for

Saturday morning, but if you prefer you may remain behind and we will go for a ride," she said with a soft chuckle.

"That would be delightful," Kara responded.

She was about to make another comment when the door opened and Lisa said, "There you are. We thought you had disappeared on us."

"Just enjoying a smoke and the sounds of the night with our hostess," Kara replied.

"We thought we might play some cards in the parlor and do some catching up before heading off to bed," Lisa suggested.

"Thanks again for the smoke," Sasha said as Kara stood to join her friends.

"You are welcome," Kara said with a smile and she disappeared into the house.

Sasha finished the cigarette, and then walked into the kitchen to find Marie preparing for the next day's meals. She could hear the chatter and soft laughter of her guests as she watched Marie move gracefully around the kitchen.

"Can you believe how much Miss Stewart looks like Milly?" Marie asked, trying to gauge the response of her friend and employer.

"I was completely taken aback when she turned around while she stood by the portrait," Sasha said. "It was as if for a moment Milly had returned, young and full of life as ever," she said with just a hint of sadness in her voice.

"She appears to be a very sweet young woman too," Marie said with a coy expression on her face.

Sasha gave a short laugh. "You are a marvel of a woman, Marie," Sasha said and with a soft touch to the woman's shoulder, she walked out of the kitchen and into the parlor.

Sasha sat before the keys at the baby grand and let her fingers brush across them as her mind became lost in a cloud of Brahms and Beethoven, playing each delicate piece from memory. Playing music relaxed Sasha, the concentration taking her mind off the fire in her stomach, intensified by the appearance of the beautiful Kara.

After Milly's death, Sasha had played less and less. Playing the baby grand in the parlor brought back memories of their youth in Europe and their life together at Sugarland. Sasha frequently felt a connection with Milly as she played, her fingers stroking the keys lightly as she remembered the softness of Milly's skin.

She was deep in memory tonight as she played, her eyes closed as Milly danced in front of her eyes, and she smiled to herself as she watched her lover.

An hour had passed since she began playing; her mind focused on the music, when Sasha opened her eyes and saw Kara standing in the doorway watching her play. Sasha fixed her eyes on Kara and quietly said, "Join me."

"You play so beautifully," Kara said as she sat in a chair across from Sasha. She found herself reluctant to break away from gazing into the woman's enchanting eyes.

"Thank you," Sasha said as she released Kara's eyes, permitting her to watch how sensually her fingertips brushed across the piano keys.

'I could be stroking your breasts like this,' Sasha planted in Kara's mind.

She watched, as Kara's nipples grew hard under the soft fabric of her blouse and a flush rose to her cheeks.

"Do you play?" Sasha quietly asked.

"Yes, but not nearly as well as you," Kara admitted.

"Join me," Sasha again beckoned and Kara slid onto the bench beside her, the warmth of her thigh spreading into Sasha.

Sasha placed her hand lightly on Kara's thigh as she began to play.

"It has been a long time and I am afraid I am a trifle rusty," Kara apologized as Sasha began to stroke her thigh.

"Relax, you are doing just fine," Sasha whispered into Kara's ear.

Kara softly sighed as she breathed in the rich cologne Sasha wore and closed her eyes to concentrate on the piece she was playing. Sasha noted the heartbeat again pulsing in Kara's neck and brazenly allowed her tongue to trail up the length of her jugular until her lips came to rest atop the pulse. Kara's body shivered at the touch of Sasha's tongue and a soft moan escaped her lips.

She softly kissed Kara's neck and listened quietly as Kara finished the piece she was playing.

"Beautiful," Sasha said when Kara's fingers played the final note and she turned toward Sasha.

"You should play more often," Sasha continued, as she looked into the deep blue of Kara's eyes.

"I know," Kara admitted. "The music is very relaxing and gives me much pleasure,".

"Maybe you will play again before you leave," Sasha suggested, "but for now I recommend you retire as Lisa has a big day planned for you tomorrow," Sasha said as she stood and led Kara to her room, parting with a wish for her guest to have sweet dreams. Sasha could feel Kara's eyes watching her as she walked down the hall toward the stairway and her room.

†

Sasha started up her computer and busied herself updating the business accounts while she listened to the sounds of the sleeping house. Shortly after midnight, she walked outside, picking up another of the cigarettes Kara had left on the porch. She had forgotten how much she enjoyed smoking and marveled at the taste as she listened to the sounds of the bayou. Clouds passed quickly in front of an almost full moon and she sighed then returned inside the house in search of sleep.

As she passed each of the rooms, she could hear the soft heartbeats and slow breathing of their sleeping occupants. A strange sound caught her ear as she neared Cindy's room and she quickly recognized the sound as the rapid heartbeat of a baby.

Smiling, Sasha walked on and stood in front of Kara's room. She silently passed through the door and looked down onto the bed where Kara slept. A soft, full breast was uncovered and a bare thigh exposed as well, revealing that Kara dozed naked on the cool sheets. Sasha watched as Kara's hand moved in her sleep to cover her breast and she slipped into Kara's dream.

Kara's dream was as vivid to Sasha as if it were reality, and she observed as her hands and mouth covered Kara's body, arousing the sleeping beauty with soft touches and nibbles. Kara's hands moved on her breasts with the exact motions Sasha was using in her dream and Sasha watched as she arched her back, begging for a firmer touch. She could hear the soft moans that were escaping Kara's lips and she resisted the temptation to give herself pleasure as she eavesdropped on Kara's dream.

Instead, she quietly turned away and retired to her room for dreams of her own.

About the Author

Ali Spooner

Ali Spooner is a native of Florida, currently living and working in Memphis, TN. Home for Ali is Pensacola, Florida where she has a partner of twenty years, one son and a grandchild that has her wrapped completely around her little finger. Her other children are all four legged, three dogs and two cats, and my dearest companion in Memphis, Rascal, a rescued tiger kitten named after my favorite country group.

A true daughter of the South, Ali enjoy spinning stories about the South, the strong, but gentle women and creatures that make it a wondrous place to live.

As an "Indie" author, Ali has been writing for many years as a hobby, and after a cancer diagnosis in 2010, she decided to take a leap and start self-publishing and has published over a dozen stories. Ali's characters range from cowgirls and psychics, to a healthy dose of supernatural beings. She has written stand-alone titles and series. Ali frequently writes several stories at a time, depending on which characters are bouncing around loudest in her head.

Ali is an avid reader and her other hobbies include photography, outdoor activities and watching college sports.

Other Books from Affinity

Beginning of the End—Alane Hotchkin What happens when life doesn't go exactly as you planned and you must protect others from your own fate? Escaping a horrific childhood, Nikki longed to find happily ever after in adulthood. What she found was Hell. Or did it find her? Finding the courage to break the cycle of betrayal, she opens her heart one last time. Alex lived a childhood others dreamed of. Her father never once denied the young rebel a thing. All her life she dreamed of protecting others; to follow in her father's footsteps. Soon though she learned sex and fists made the most powerful of weapons. Alex controls the women in her life through fear and sex, will breaking the cycle be too much to overcome? Will loving Nikki be enough to change her, or is Alex beyond help?

Alex would give Nikki the world, but at what price? When a person's tightly controlled reality snaps what then…? This is the Beginning of the End for one of them and the ultimate sacrifice for the other. But who is who in this game of life?

Galveston 1900: Swept Away—Linda Crist On September 7-8, 1900, the island of Galveston, Texas, was destroyed by a hurricane, or 'tropical cyclone', as it was called in those days. This story is a fictional account of Mattie and Rachel, two women who lived there, and their lives during the time of the 'great storm'. Forced to flee from her family at a young age, Rachel Travis finds a home and livelihood on the island of Galveston. Independent, friendly, and yet often lonely, only one other person knows the dark secret that haunts her. Madeline "Mattie" Crockett is trapped in a loveless marriage, convinced that her fate is sealed. She never dares to dream of true happiness, until Rachel Travis comes walking into her life.   As emotions come to light, the storm of Mattie's marriage converges with the very real hurricane. Can they survive, and build the life they both dream of?

This second edition of one of Linda Crist's best-loved novels maintains the original story, while incorporating some reader-pleasing passages that were cut from the first edition. As an added bonus, the short story "Something to Celebrate" is included at the end of the novel, detailing further adventures of Rachel and Mattie.

Rapture: Sins of the Sinners—A. C. Henley & Fran Heckrotte   A serial killer is targeting young lesbians throughout the state of Texas.Texas Ranger Cochetta Lovejoy is assigned to the case. Convinced she knows who is committing the murders, Ranger Lovejoy is willing to do whatever it takes to put the perpetrator behind bars--even if it means stretching the limits of the law by manipulating the judicial system. Detective Agnes Kelly-Elliott is one of Ft. Worth Police Department's finest investigators.   When Ranger Lovejoy appears on the crime scene of a recent murder, Agnes fears a dark secret that, if revealed, could destroy her family ties, and end her career. This is a dark, gritty, graphic tale of desire gone awry, and flawed characters looking for redemption in all the wrong places.

Till There Was You—S. Anne Gardner   Julia is a woman used to power and is not afraid to use it or impose her will to get her way. She appears to have the world but a part of her is empty and cold as a frozen tundra. Julia rides in the mornings to clear her head and to make plans for what she is about to set in motion. Theodora, known as Teddy, is trying to put together a marriage filled with uncertainties. She felt once upon a time that she would have a great love but that has eluded her. One morning these two women meet and from the first instance, it is explosive. The attraction is undeniable, the fears very real and the end without question will change them both forever.

Denial—Jackie Kennedy   Time spent in Somalia has Doctor Celeste Cameron accustomed to living and working in a war zone. Coming back home to America, Celeste is glad to see the end of the peril she has been in—or so she thinks. Danger seems to follow Celeste and she finds it in the shape of Amy. What Celeste feels for Amy scares her more than anything she has faced in war zones. Amy has the same feelings, but is in denial and vows to marry Josh, Celeste's twin brother, no matter what. When fate brings them together again, will they give in to their mutual attraction or will they once again deny what they feel.

In Name Only—JM Dragon—Sequel to The Fix-it Girl   Can an agreement forged out of necessity actually work?

'55 Ford—**Erin O'Reilly**   Andrea McBride, the author of four books, wants to find someone to restore an old '55 Ford truck that she inherited in a real estate purchase. She will only settle for the best and finds RJ

Whittaker who many proclaim to be the best restorer among millions.

An Affair of Love—S. Anne Gardner From a dark past, a forbidden love, a secret comes. Among the confusion and the chaos of an unwanted reality, two women find something they neither want nor can deny.

Desert Heat—Dannie Marsden For Luce Diamond, an undercover policewoman, her life is in shambles. Her longtime lover left her and an automobile accident that resulted in a child's death haunts her.

Taming the Wolff—Del Robertson ONLY ONE WOMAN...HAS THE POWER...TO TAME THE WOLFF...

Private Dancer—TJ Vertigo Reece Corbett grew up on the mean streets on New York City, abused, used and in trouble with the law. Faith Ashford grew up wealthy, with all the creature comforts that money provides. When they meet fireworks begin.

Miriam and Esther—Sherry Barker Miriam thought her life would play out in the bustling metropolis of Dallas, but after a life-changing accident, she moves to the small town of Cool Lake, Texas to get her head on straight and regain her senses.

McKee—**A.C. Henley** Private Investigator Quinlan McKee has returned to Los Angeles after a three-year absence, only to find herself embroiled in a world of child slavery and police corruption.

Bailey's Run—Ali Spooner Bailey Chambers mourns the loss of her lover, Nessa, in an unsolved carjacking. When Tommy, Bailey's brother becomes a victim of a gay bashing, Bailey assumes his case will be handled the same way as her lover's—lackadaisically.

Desi Dexter assigned to Tommy's case, feels Bailey's disdain toward her and her partner. Through tenacious police work, Desi, is able to uncover the reason for Bailey's attitude, and convinces her that she is sincere in solving the case.

Mutual attraction sparks, and before they can move forward with their fledging romance, Desi, and her partner Braxton, uncover the presence of a serial killer.

What will happen to Bailey, when, Desi, becomes engrossed in another case, can their relationship survive?

E-Books, Print, Free e-books
Visit our website for more publications available online.

www.affinityebooks.com

Affinity E-Book Press NZ LTD

Canterbury, New Zealand

Registered Company 2517228